"I have lea... medium abilities to deliver messages of hope and guidance to my clients. It is my absolute honor to be a part of helping them to see their best self."

-Kenna Smith, CHt.

"Kenna has continually blown my mind in the few months since I have had the pleasure of meeting her. She has an amazing intuition and is always bang on! I would highly recommend her. Be ready to be stunned by her accuracy and insight!"

-Donna H.

"I have had a couple of readings with Kenna and I found her to be an extraordinarily talented psychic medium. I went to her seeking guidance and clarity and I got exactly what I needed at the time. Her insights are exceptional and her messages delivered with heart."

-Ali S.

"I can truly say that Kenna changed my life. Not only did she seem to know me inside and out, she was incredibly accurate at predicting events yet to unfold in my life. I have never seen someone with such a beautiful energy surrounding her. Because of her, I am now exploring my spirituality, connecting to myself, earth and even my spirit guides, I have never been happier."

-Kaitland S.

"A session with Kenna isn't just a reading, it is a life changing experience. Her amazing gift is matched by her loving personality. She delivers the most accurate messages and you leave a session with her filled with hope and inspiration."

-Liane F.

Kenna Smith has a YouTube channel; Psychic Kenna; where she regularly posts videos of her experiences. She also conducts workshops and seminars for people who wish to grow their own psychic gifts. Kenna is a keynote speaker and would love to be a part of your next conference or gathering.

MY PSYCHIC MEDIUM MIND

A journey into
the thinplaces
and beyond.

KENNA SMITH, CHt.

This book is an original publication of ThinPlace Visionary.

MY PSYCHIC MEDIUM MIND

A ThinPlace Visionary Book / published by arrangement with the author

Copyright ©2018
Kenna Smith, CHt
Author Photo Copyright © 2018 by ThinPlace Visionary

For information address:
ThinPlace Visionary
3765 Melrose Rd. Qualicum Beach, BC Canada V9K 1V3

The website address is:
http://www.psychickenna.com

Note for Librarians: A cataloguing record for this book is available from Library and Archives Canada at www.collectionscanada.ca/amicus/index-e.html

ISBN – 978-0-2285-0-131-2

Printed in Canada
FIRST CHOICE BOOKS

www.firstchoicebooks.ca
Victoria, BC

10 9 8 7 6 5 4 3 2 1

"For my biggest fan, my inspiration and greatest love; my husband Skyler.

For Nate, Liv and Trey for sitting through all my stories, encouraging me to follow my dreams and never give up!!

For my best friend, Deena who came to me moments after her passing to tell me to be a hero."

CONTENTS

ACKNOWLEDGMENTS

I wish to thank God, my friends and my family for helping me to be the best version of myself. A huge thank you to all of my amazing, sparkly clients for sharing their lives with me and allowing me to be a part of their story. For encouraging me to write this book that has long been sitting in the back of my psychic medium mind. Each and every one of you has made an impact on my life that has ultimately led me to this moment. I am forever grateful for all the lessons learned, the laughter, the tears and the many bricks to my head! This book is a culmination of my own personal experiences and journey of self discovery. Thanks for sharing your time and yourselves with me.

A special thank you to my husband Skyler, for being my biggest fan and always encouraging me to believe in my abilities and myself. You are my best friend and I love you absolutely!

My Son Nathan: You are an incredible person that I am proud to call my son. Thank you for your unwavering support through all of our adventures. You have always been honest with me, honorable in your actions and through it all, you make me laugh. I love you!

My Nephew Trey: Your magical mind and deep thinking have blessed me more than you will ever know.

Thank you for listening to my endless stories, I love you so much Bubby!

Olivia: You are so beautiful inside and out. You are an important part of the success of this book and your encouragement and excitement has meant the world to me!

Deena: I miss you so much and think of you often. As I was writing this book you were my inspiration to keep going no matter what. Your courage and grace in life and in death inspires me to be the Hero you always knew I was. I will see you in the thinplaces my friend!

My New Smith Family: Thank you to each and every one of you that are a part of this crazy, huge extended family. You made me a part of your tribe and gave me back the sense of belonging that I was missing. Your love is overwhelming and amazing! Looking forward to many more family get togethers and shenanigans!

My Girls: Liane, Holly, Janet and Tracy; there are not enough words to express how much you all mean to me. Your support and listening ears have made this dream of mine a reality. I could not ask for better women to be in my circle with me. Go out and shine brightly and the world will notice!

Sue Sue & Brian: You are gold! You helped bring me out of the darkness, showed me I was loved, led me to my deepest faith, helped me to be a better human and loved my child and I unconditionally. It is not an exaggeration to say that you saved my life and gave me

• • •

II

the hope to grow into the person I am today. I will forever be grateful.

Barry & Nancy: You have been my friends, my spiritual advisors, and supporters. Barry your intellect and caring nature has both challenged me, infuriated me and blessed me beyond words. Nancy, I just love you to bits! There was never anything we couldn't talk about or laugh at or cry over. You are a true friend.

Jeff Richards: You are a gifted medium and teacher. I could not have asked for a better mentor to guide me to the next stage of my adventure. Your ability to motivate me and your belief in my gifts has set my feet firmly on this path. Thank you.

Chelsea & Jay: Chelsea, you were the catalyst for this book. Sitting at the counter that day when you said, "You already have a book written", was a light bulb moment. Jay, your willingness to do whatever was necessary to give me the space and a beautiful home to write in was appreciated. You are both lovely souls and I am grateful.

Rose, Angie & Donna: Thank you ladies for believing in me and giving me space to bring light into the world. You have built up my confidence and been wonderful supporters of all things light!

Georgina: You are the most radiant, lovely woman I have had the honor to know. You opened your world to allow me to teach and learn. I am grateful for your graciousness. Keep connecting the Lightworkers in that magical way you do!

• • •

Jeannie & Richard: You came into my life in a most delightful way and brought transformation on such a deep level. I thank you both for seeing my light before I ever did. Your gift is in leading others to be the truest form of themselves. You bring sparkle, joy and infinite wisdom to my world.

The following people I have been blessed to have in my life over the years. Their influence has been like a seed planted that keeps growing and producing beautiful flowers. Each and every one of you has been an important part of my adventure! Thanks for being my friends.

Ethel & Bruce Henry, Cathy & Brian Kaardal, Tammy Willow, Jay Bettis, Lori & Todd Labrador, Randy & Debbie McCartenay, Nina Dow, Carmen MacKenzie, The Melanson Clan, Norm & Jane Herbin, Dave & Debbie Tombe, the amazing Kelly family, my Vineyard family, my Lambrick Park Church family, Lion of Judah family, Don Crawford, Joan Knott, Jean Hersom, Mike & Moira Jones, Darren & Kathleen Stone, Jackie & Todd Munro, Kerry Harvey, Kell & Lori Frandsen, the "Takraw" boys and their families, Teri Kerr, Bruce & Lorraine Freissen, my Hypnotherapy family, and Dr. Phillip Ney. There are so many more people that I have been blessed to have in my life. If you know me, you are valued and consider your name written here as well!!

PREFACE

When I was in high school, English was my favorite subject. I would write for hours upon hours. I kept journals for most of my life, wrote several amateur plays. Writing short stories was my favorite thing to do. I always dreamed that one day I would write a "real" book that would make a difference in peoples lives. My own life was chaotic and tumultuous most of the time and writing offered an escape for me. I have always had an intense curiosity to adventure my way through life, learning and experiencing as much as I could. I constantly moved around, changed jobs, went to school, travelled and met as many people as I could. For years I thought there was something wrong with me. I could not seem to just settle into one thing and be content.

One year, my son bought me a sign that was hand painted with the words, "Not all those who wander are lost." It literally changed my thinking from believing that my thirst for adventure was a character flaw, into realizing that I was living my life to the fullest! It is because of all the people I have been honored to meet along the way, all the adventures I have participated in and the many life lessons I have learned that has given me the confidence to write this book.

I had a few ideas for different books floating around in my head for years, but every time I thought it was time to go ahead and start writing I felt like I was swimming through peanut butter. Nothing but struggle and getting nowhere! One day, I was in my kitchen visiting with my neighbor. She was asking me some questions about how I do what I do. I explained to her my process of meditating on a client and psychic journalling. She was fascinated and asked how many pages of these notes I had. I pulled out my stack of twenty or so journals with the hundreds of readings I had conducted. She looked at me and said, "Well, there is your book right there! It is already written!" Something inside of me just clicked and I realized she was right. All the while I was trying to come up with some unique and interesting ideas for a novel and I had it all right there in front of me the whole time! My Psychic Medium Mind is a culmination of years of giving readings, the outcomes of those readings and the understanding I have gained as a result.

I walked through my life always aware that I was different than the people around me. Not better, just different. I was born with the ability to see energy moving and to communicate with spirits of people that have crossed over. As you can imagine this meant that I had some pretty unusual stories and experiences.

I found that when people learned of my abilities they were always so curious and had lots of questions. I hope to answer many of these questions as well as provide my unique insights into the world of spirit. I have been blessed to give hundreds of personal readings over the years. I love to impart to others how to embrace and grow their own intuitive gifts, and have had the privilege to teach varied courses on this subject. In addition to being a full time Psychic Medium, I am also a Clinical Hypnotherapist. I am motivated by the idea that my small voice can cause a ripple effect in this current time and place that will change lives, and bring hope and acceptance into our world. God gave us all a light. I hope that by being vulnerable and allowing my light to shine brightly that I will encourage you to do the same.

PART 1

HOW DO YOU DO THAT?

INTRODUCTION

Where do I begin? I suppose the best place to begin is at the beginning. Like most people I was born into a fairly average family. My father worked in the logging industry and my mother was a stay-at-home mom. I have an older sister and a younger brother, which makes me the middle child. Although I was born into a typical family, my life was anything but typical. From a very early age, I knew that I wasn't like anybody else. I grew up feeling different, alone, misunderstood and isolated.

I am hesitant to talk about my childhood, as it feels I could write a whole separate book just to cover that topic. Perhaps my next book will be about that complicated subject! This book is about my journey into discovering the amazing gifts that I've been given and what I have learned along the way. That journey began when I was a young child.

Ever since I can remember, I have had the ability to see the world around me vibrating and moving. I can see energy in people, animals and all living things. I assumed that everyone saw the world the same way I did. I often became over stimulated by peoples energy and the constant ebb and flow of my environment. I would retreat into my own space to quiet my mind and recharge my own energies. Of course, at the time I didn't realize that was what I was doing. I simply understood that I needed to get away from everyone and everything.

• • •

When I was in my own private world, I realized that it wasn't just the energy of the things around me that I could see but also the energies of people that had crossed over as well. I remember many days sitting alone in my room having conversations with spirits from the other side. I called them my friends. I believe that was what my young mind could accept them to be. I understand now that this was the beginning of my coming to know my many spirit guides. They have always been there to keep me safe, protect me and teach me.

I endured many years of abuse as a child and during this time I suspected my guides were there to help me survive. That may sound strange to many people, but all I can say is they were there to take my mind off what was happening in my day-to-day life. They genuinely were my best friends and still are to this day.

Many nights as I slept, I would dream that I was flying all over the world. Specifically, I would be sitting in a lawn chair and peddling my feet. The faster I peddled the higher I would fly. When I wanted to coast, I simply stuck my legs straight out in front of me and I would coast along. I would travel throughout my neighborhood, my friends' homes, my town and eventually all over the world. I assumed I had a really active imagination and dream life.

I have since come to understand that I was astral travelling. Many times I would go to someones' house and know exactly where things were, even if I had never physically been there before. I remember once, describing a place in Istanbul, where I bought a beautiful fabric cloth.

• • •

I drew the pattern and showed it to my grade school teacher. He told me that he thought it was a beautiful drawing and asked where I had seen that particular pattern. I told him I had seen it in my dreams when I went to a marketplace in Istanbul. A few days later he came back to school with a photograph of a middle eastern shop that had displays of many beautiful fabrics. In the photo was the exact same pattern that I had drawn. I thought this was pretty cool and I recall my teacher being a bit freaked out.

There was an incident once when I was in my teens. I was walking home from school and felt strongly that I needed to get home quickly because my sister was in trouble. I ran in the door and told my mom that she needed to go and pick up my sister, she needed her help. My mom replied that my sister was fine and that I should calm down. I insisted that she go to the school and pick up my sister. Again, she told me to calm down and stop being so dramatic. A few minutes later the phone rang and it was my sister. She had gotten into a big fight with her boyfriend and needed my mom to come and pick her up. I will never forget the look on my mother's face when she looked at me and said, "I don't how you did that, but I don't want to talk about it again." In that moment I felt like there was something wrong with me. I put a wall up that day and never shared my gifts with my family again. Upon reflection, I understood that my mother was just frightened and never meant to have such a lasting impact on me.

As a child I was very emotional, and felt things very intensely. My siblings and parents were not expressive or sensitive in the same way that I was. I was often referred to as, "the dramatic child" or "the drama queen." This hurt me deeply, but more than that, it taught me that expressing my emotions or talking about my abilities was a flaw in me and not something to be celebrated. I began a downward spiral into masking my true nature and adapting to whatever situations I found myself in. I became a chameleon that could mimic any event or person that I was around. I became so good at this, that by the time I was in my twenties I had no idea who I truly was.

I tried very hard to shut out the voices in my head, the vibrations I could see, and the spirits that would constantly come looking for my help. I didn't know anyone that experienced what I did and had no one to talk to or learn from. I began using drugs and drinking to try and numb myself. I became depressed and struggled with anxiety.

During this time, I became pregnant with my son. I made a conscious decision that I wanted to be the best possible mother that I could be. I started by cutting off all my addictive behaviors and focusing on motherhood. I wish my story was different and that I could say that everything was fine after that, but it wasn't. Now that I didn't have anything left to numb my senses, all of my abilities came flooding in like a tidal wave.

This began ten years of what I called, the dark years. I became deeply depressed and suicidal. I was hospitalized many times and medicated to the point that I felt nothing. The doctors diagnosed me with many disorders over the years. They treated me with medication, hospitalization, electroshock therapy and group therapy. I was eventually diagnosed with PTSD and told that I would have this disability for the rest of my life. During this time, I had many hundreds of spirits, both from the light and the dark pushing their way towards me. I felt attacked and overwhelmed and wanted it all to stop.

I decided that if the doctors and the medical establishment couldn't help me and drugs or alcohol weren't the answer, then perhaps the church could be my refuge. I began attending church with a wonderful lady who would become like a mother to me and my son. I felt welcomed and understood for the first time in my life. People would talk about spirits and hearing voices as if this was all normal. They explained to me that I was hearing from God. I spent many years going to church every Sunday. I attended prayer groups, volunteered in my community and did missions work around the world. I learned so much from these wonderful people. I developed a close personal relationship with God and still talk with him constantly. He talks to me just as much. Throughout my time in the church I used my gifts openly to help others and bring healing. My insights and visions were welcomed and encouraged. My skills began to grow again and this time I felt I had more control. As I healed in this loving and caring environment I grew to understand that it was okay to be different and that God made us all uniquely special.

The more I used my gifts, the clearer it became to me that my abilities were indeed a gift from God. I could bring light to people in the darkness. With more clarity came the understanding that my time in the church was coming to an end.

• • •

I remember the exact Sunday that my pastor and friend was giving a sermon on being authentic. It hit me really hard, because I knew that I wasn't being authentic. Although I believed my gifts came from God, I knew that it wasn't just God that I was hearing from. I knew that I was communicating with spirits of people that had crossed over, my spirit guides, I was reading energy and talking to God. When I communicated this to my pastor, I understood this to be outside of the beliefs of the church. I recognized that my Christian family was instrumental in my healing and they will forever have a special place in my heart. It was devastating for me to leave behind the church in order to live as my authentic self.

When I left the church behind, I stepped into a new phase in my journey. I fully embraced the gifts that I'd been given. I now have an amazing husband, a wonderful mentor, supportive and loving friends and no longer feel the need to try to please everyone. I am just me. I am a little quirky, I talk to dead people, I love God, I shine brightly and I hope to bring more light to the world.

My dream is that this book, my story and the lessons that I've learned will bring an understanding that the world is so much bigger than what we see with just our eyes. There is hope, there is a God and our loved ones live on in spirit. After many hundreds of readings, psychic experiences and spirit communications I have learned a few things about Heaven. I am excited to impart that knowledge and understanding. I will disclose to you my process and how I do what I do. I have chosen several readings to share with you and I hope that you will also learn and grow from these experiences.

MY PROCESS

People often ask me, "How do you do that?." I will do my best to explain exactly how I do that and how I developed my individual process. This is my process and I recognize that everyone has a way of connecting to their intuition and it is unique and specific to them. I have developed my system over the years and through many readings and it works for me. I would encourage you to develop your own method of listening to your intuition, communicating with your spirit guides and praying to God.

Over the years my process for tapping into my gifts has changed and evolved as I have changed and evolved. In the beginning when I was quite young, I really had no process all. If I had a vision, an image or some knowledge, I believed it was my duty to share it immediately. In my mind, I felt that everyone would want to know what I had to share. I was young and a bit naïve in my belief system. There were many times when I may have hurt people inadvertently by simply speaking my mind without first asking for their permission or asking God and my guides whether now was the time to speak. As a result of this, I experienced a lot of negativity and rejection. I found that people seemed a bit awkward around me, as if they were afraid of what I was going to say. I felt misunderstood and believed that what I had to offer was not wanted.

As I matured and became more self-aware I started asking myself the question, "Should I share this information now or is it just for me to know?". I didn't realize at the time, I wasn't really asking myself, I was praying to God and talking to my guides. When I began going to church I realized that my abilities were necessary and welcomed by this new group of people in my life. One of the greatest lessons I learned from my pastor was the importance of testing the words that I was given. In addition, he taught me to remember that God was my authority and to ask him for permission to share the messages. This may sound restrictive to some people, but I have to say for me, it gave me a sense of order and helped me to realize the great responsibility of the gifts I had been given. There is something to be said for being accountable and working with honor.

As I grew confident in my abilities to help people by sharing my visions and the words that were given to me, my skills also advanced in strength. It was during this time that I began to put some separation between myself and the church. It was an incredibly difficult decision as going to church and being a part of that community had been my life for over twenty years. Change is never easy and there's a grieving process that happens. As I grieved the loss of my friends and teachers, I realized I was very much alone and without counsel. I knew the value of having someone who has walked a mile in your shoes to talk to and learn from. So I decided to seek out a mentor of my own who was a psychic medium and understood the struggles and conflicts within my mind in regards to leaving my church family behind and embracing my true self. In the way the universe usually works in my life, that door opened wide and my mentor found me.

• • •

He taught me many things. He taught me the importance of meditation and focused thought. He taught me the need for protection for myself, my environment, the people I work with and the people I love. He taught me about integrity and honesty. He taught me about intention and believing in what I do. Throughout my time with him I began to develop a specific process for growing my gifts and focusing them. At the same time, I went back to school and became a Certified Clinical Hypnotherapist.

I love my work as a Hypnotherapist and am surprised at how my choice of career and my natural gifts work so well together. I developed several self-hypnosis meditations for protection, focusing my intuitive gifts and increasing my ability to communicate with spirit.

These meditations have become a part of my daily process. Every morning when I wake I do approximately twenty minutes of yoga to prepare my body for the day and a half hour of self hypnosis meditation to prepare my mind. I spend time every day outside in nature with my animals and the earth. This prepares my spirit to be connected.

If I am meeting with clients that day, I will spend more time in meditation focusing solely on their energy and the messages I am receiving for them. Most times I have never met my clients beforehand. I communicate only through email or phone messages to book the appointment. So that when I am focusing on their energy I rely completely on my gifts and not my powers of observation. During my meditation time I will surround myself with light, wash away any negative energies, ground myself in the earth, and fill myself with the energy of all creation and the Holy Spirit before I open myself to reading others energy and connecting with spirit.

When I am fully prepared to open myself up, my gifts just seem to take over. I can see others energy like a river flowing forwards and backwards. I journal all that I see and all the impressions that I get from following my client's energy. In addition, I ask my guides to provide me with any information that they think is necessary for my client to hear and again I journal exactly what I'm getting. It is important for me not to over analyze or try to make sense of the messages that I'm given. These messages are not for me, they are for my clients. I believe the best thing to do is to allow my clients to discern the meanings for themselves. I am human however, and occasionally I overthink things and miss the mark. The next step in my process is to be still and listen to the voice of God as he often has information to share.

I write until my intuition leads me to stop. When I am done, I close my journal and thank God and my guides for communicating with me and helping me to help others. During the sessions with my clients I usually start with my notes. I allow a reading to go in whatever direction feels best as long as the energy is clean and clear. I protect my space by smudging and praying over my area before and after each encounter.

My mediumship is expressed slightly differently and my process with this is also different. In the beginning, spirits would come to me constantly and persistently, and I felt that I had no control to make them stop. With experience and teaching I learned that I was in control and could turn on and off my spirit communication. It took a lot of practice and a few unusual techniques, but I am now able to manage my ability to communicate with spirit. Specifically, I have designed a mental process where I picture myself putting on a pair of glasses. I called them, "God Goggles." When I want to communicate with spirit and see the other side, I imagine putting on my God Goggles. When I am done and want a break, I take them off. I realize it sounds a bit simplistic, but it took me a couple of years to really develop this practice to the point that I feel confident with being able to turn the communication on and off.

Prior to a reading, I will put my God Goggles on and let the universe know I am open to communicating with spirit and I am in control and will only allow positive entities to communicate with me. I use all five of my senses when communicating with spirit. I can see them as clearly as I can see a person standing in front of me. Occasionally, they are more difficult to see, but I can usually make out their age and gender. I hear spirits. They can and will talk to me in full sentences if they are able. If they don't have enough energy to do that, they will use symbols, pictures and even pop culture images to communicate. I can also feel their emotions. I'm sure you can imagine how awkward this could be during a reading if a husband who is deeply in love with his wife shares his emotions with me. I will often gaze lovingly at my clients, weep silently and even be sarcastic with them. I can smell and taste during a reading and find that spirit often communicates this way. If I touch an item belonging to someone who is crossed over I feel connected to the energy of the person who's passed on and have an easier time communicating with them.

• • •

During a reading I like to remind my clients that spirit is here to communicate with them and not me. I am simply the medium. I encourage them to communicate with me during the process as I find it allows the spirits to communicate more freely and powerfully. What I do is not a trick and I am never trying to fool anyone. It is an amazing gift to be able to witness that moment when someone realizes that their loved ones truly do live on in spirit. It never gets old and always, always blesses me and encourages me to keep doing what I do

I will share with you my journal notes from specific readings as well as a synopsis of the reading itself. Please remember that these notes are taken before I have met with anyone and are written purely from my intuition, conversations with God, my spirit guides and my ability to read energy. I have changed all names and distinguishing information to honour my client's privacy. My desire is that by sharing my process and my readings, I will be able to impact more people. We live in a very physical world, but there is a spiritual world all around us. With eyes to see and an open heart there is hope and clarity for each one of us.

PROTECT YOURSELF

$\mathcal{S}$piritual Protection is something that everyone should know how to do, regardless of your religious beliefs (or lack of). It encompasses far more than just ghosts & spirits. Negativity in any form can be damaging to the human energy field or aura. Fear, anger, depression, negative people, places, arguments and more actually create negative energy that can cling to you or build up in your home and cause problems over time. Spiritual cleansings are very important, for yourself and your home. As a psychic medium I do spiritual protection rituals daily to keep my energy clean and my light strong. I have included a few of my favorite techniques and I want to encourage you to do your research and find some that fit best for you. We are all different and our protection needs are just as unique!

1) Imbuing Objects With Intent

To "charge" something means that you are infusing it with energy and your intention. You can charge things like jewelry, to hold a certain intent. Metals hold a charge very well and for a long time. For example, you can "charge" rings or necklaces with prosperity and success energy then wear them to a job interview. Will this guarantee you the job? Of course not. But you are stating your intent to the universe, and therefore you are putting certain energies into motion. It's all about your intent and the energy you put into it. There are instructions on how to go about doing this practice in the reference section at the back of this book.

2) Crystals & Rocks

Certain crystals and stones also carry spiritual protection properties. Here is a short list of the most common ones:

Agate, amber, amethyst, black onyx, citrine, coral, emerald, garnet, obsidian (apache tears), ruby, tourmaline.

You can charge your gemstones with intent and either carry them with you, place them around your home, or purchase jewelry that contains stones with the properties you want, and wear them.

3) Angels & Spirit Guides

Ask for spiritual and physical protection from your angels and guides. That is what they are there for. Each of us is assigned certain angels and guides before we are born. Their job is to protect us, comfort and guide us, and to work with us in living our most productive life possible here on earth. But remember that they cannot interfere with our free will. We must invite their help if we want it.

You can ask for their protection daily for general purposes, or you can ask when you have an immediate need for protection. But keep in mind that although they are assigned to us, they are not our slaves. They help us because they want to. Respect and gratitude should always be the context in which you request their assistance. Be

• • •
17

thankful for their presence in your life and know that you are never alone.

I often get asked, "What is the difference between angels and spirit guides?" Typically, Angels are beings of light that have not incarnated on earth before. They work closely with God and humans, helping to uplift, encourage and comfort us when we are in need. They may also come to deliver important messages to us, or to facilitate some specific healing we may need. They also provide inspiration in the form of ideas for certain projects we may be here to complete. Spirit Guides are usually human souls who have incarnated on earth many times, and have reached a highly enlightened stage of development, and now work closely with humans on earth to help guide, teach and enlighten us in our spiritual growth.

There are subtle differences between angels and spirit guides, and sometimes their duties and characteristics may overlap. Some people may be more comfortable referring to all their guides as "Angels", whereas some prefer to discern between the two types of spiritual helpers. The main thing to remember is that both beings are here to help guide us and make our earthly experience as meaningful and efficient as possible.

How do we begin working with our angels and guides? We are already working with them, whether consciously or not. Our guides are working with us almost constantly, even if we are not aware of it.

They come into our dreams to convey information or to help us work through problems we may be having. At various times our angels and guides can also whisper things to us in our waking hours, or during sleep.

• • •

We may hear this consciously, or not. How many times have you been struggling with some problem for days, suddenly inspiration strikes, and you know the answer? You feel amazement that you didn't think of it before now. Very often this knowledge comes from our angels or guides.

If we want to work with them, they will expect us to work. This can mean many different things for each of us. We may be encouraged to alter our lifestyle, or change careers, or work harder and more often in our development. We will be urged to shed the security blankets so many of us surround ourselves with. This can be anything from addictions to self- limiting thoughts and activities. But at the same time, this can be the most rewarding path you will ever set foot upon. If you will release your ego and trust that your guides truly love you and want the best for you, then you can attain so much growth and meaning in your life that it will astound you.

You can tell the difference between an actual guide and an imposter by the feelings and information you get from them. Remember that our angels and guides are highly enlightened beings that work closely with God. They are filled with light, love and compassion. They will never tell you to do anything negative, like harming yourself or others. They would never demand you do something. They would never encourage you to do or say negative things. Our guides are responsible and knowledgeable. They will encourage us to explore our abilities in a positive way. They will point us in the right direction. They will convey messages that will aid us in our spiritual growth. Their teachings will be of a positive nature, not negative.

• • •

4) Smudging and Cleansing

Negative energy can often linger in a dwelling, causing all kinds of problems from fatigue to appliance failure. If you've just moved into a new home, or if your home has a negative feel to it, it's a good idea to spiritually cleanse all unwanted influences. Do this frequently in your home and car, whether you sense negative energy or not. First clean your home and car physically, getting it as uncluttered as possible, especially in the corners. Sweep or vacuum the floors, removing all dust and dirt. You can use a smudging ritual like the one used by First Nations peoples around the world. I do this regularly and often get comments from family, friends and clients about how calm and serene my home is.

Smudging- A smoking fire meant to drive away...

Among the First Nations, smudging is a sacred ceremony meant to bring about change. Smudging helps to purify our bodies, aura and energy; cleanse ceremonial spaces and personal articles; clear the negative and attract the positive; is used to help center and balance the body, mind and spirit; and promotes healing. Our bodies are not only physical but vibrate with those invisible silent energies that come when all the elements and their medicines are working together. This is what makes smudging so powerful, using all the elements together and understanding their purpose.

- *Physical - Earth Element - Medicines*

  Cedar - wards of sickness

  Tobacco - connects us to spirit realm

  Sage - clears negative

  Sweetgrass - attracts positive

- *Mental - Air Element - Feathers*

  Because of the way the feather is constructed it can comb someone's aura or energy of blockages allowing a cleansing to happen. Call on the strength and gentleness of the feather.

- *Emotional - Water Element - Shell*

  Water cleanses the earth of all negative, quenches our thirst in times of need and brings life. It is both calm and gentle; ferocious and turbulent. It brings change.

- *Spiritual - Fire Element - Smoke*

  When fire is used to light the medicines, it awakens the existing powers to work. Bringing male energy for balance. The smoke carries the prayers to the Creator.

Common herbs used in smudging:

Sagebrush: transforms energy and brings change.
Sage: brings wisdom and is calming and healing.
Sweetgrass: attracts positive energy.
Lavender: restores balance and creates a peaceful atmosphere. Lavender also attracts loving energy and spirits.
Cedar: deeply purifying, especially for clearing negative emotions and for healing and as a way to attract positive energy. Also used to bless a home before taking residence there, a tradition dating back to the Northwest and Western Canadian Native Americans, and believed to aid clairvoyance, revive the tired mind, body, and spirit, and stimulate contact with other worlds.
Mugwort: stimulates psychic awareness and prophetic dreams. It also banishes evil spirits.
Juniper: used to purify and create a safe and sacred space.
Yerba Santa: used to purify and to set and protect boundaries.
Rosemary: a powerful healer that brings clarity to the problems.

5) White Light Visualization and Meditation

One of the most important aspects of spiritual protection is white light protection. It's very simple to do, and maybe you've even read about it or done it without knowing it. It's very effective at removing and preventing negative energy from harming you.

You begin by visualizing a bright white light hovering above you. You then imagine this light entering your body and completely permeating throughout you. This white light represents, love, kindness, positive energy and light. Imagine it pushing out or burning up any negativity that you may have picked up from others or from your own thoughts. You can visualize this light completely covering you like a protective bubble or energy field that you are in complete control over. It can stay as close or as far from you as you like. I have included the link to a 10-minute recorded visualization for you in the reference section of this book. Do not listen to this while driving or operating any machinery as it is a form of self-hypnosis. Be sure to find a nice quiet and a comfortable spot where you will not be disturbed for ten minutes and enjoy!

PART 2

MY ADVENTURES AND READINGS

ALLISON

Allison was a beautiful and reserved woman whom I could tell was very nervous. We talked for a few moments about what to expect during the reading and she seemed to settle down enough that we could begin. I started with my notes like I always do. I asked her if she was considering going to school for something administrative as I had seen this in my meditation time. She had been deciding whether to go to school to study business administration. This was one of the main questions she had come seeking guidance for. This certainly broke the ice and we began to settle into the reading. I told her that I expected she would be taking a trip up to the north of Canada this summer. She would have to travel over water to get there. I showed her a picture of two tree stumps that were cut down. I felt this was symbolic of a time in her life that was cut too short.

Allison was taking a trip to the North to visit her ancestral home and would be traveling on a ferry to get there. I knew this would be a difficult and also healing journey for her. I felt a strong connection to a necklace that Allison was wearing and mentioned to her that I felt it belonged to someone important in her life and she had a strong emotional attachment to this necklace. I also felt it was tied to the trip she was meant to take. Allison explained to me that the necklace had once belonged to her mother. She was traveling to her childhood home to

have some closure over a difficult upbringing in which her
parents had abandoned her to foster care. She did feel that

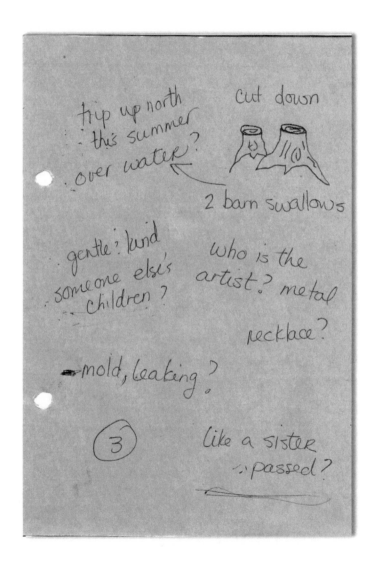

her life had been cut too short with her family and was hoping to reconnect with them.

I could see that this was a difficult subject for Allison to discuss, so I moved on in order to give her a break. I knew there would be even more emotional subjects to discuss in order for her to experience healing.

I felt that there was a strong mold problem in her home or the home of one of her children. It was causing respiratory issues. I fit the mold was hidden behind paint and not obvious, therefore the problem was going undetected. She told me there was a very strong smell of mold in her daughter's home and her granddaughter was suffering from asthma like symptoms. She had just recently asked her daughter and granddaughter to move in with her because was concerned about the health problems associated with the mold. I drew her attention to the notes where I had written that she was caring for someone else's children. We both had a laugh and she said, "I am definitely doing that and have been for a very long time."

I became aware of a spirit presence in the room and asked Allison if she was open to communicating. I always ask for permission before engaging with spirit as I feel it is important that the person I am meeting with is comfortable and wanting this communication. Allison expressed that she was open and I could tell that she was nervous and had an expectation for whom she wished to communicate with. I began to describe two women, both of them were very funny and had a wonderful sense of humor, they looked a lot alike, they had beautiful hair, were very made up and laughing together. One of the women I could sense was very connected to nature and tended to spend a lot of time alone in the woods. She was still spending a lot of time in nature while on the other side. Allison began to get emotional and tears formed in her eyes. She told me that I was describing her mother and her aunt. Her mother had lived in a very isolated community and would often go deep into the forest for hours to pick berries and roots.

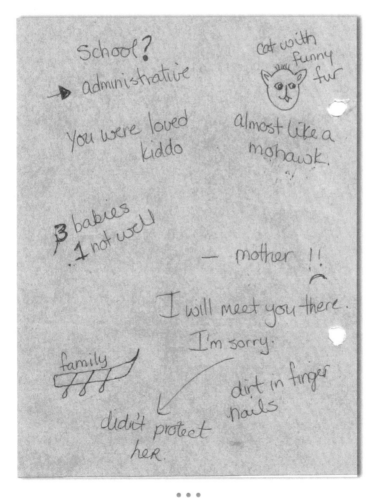

I focused all of my energy on her mother and asked her if there were any special messages that she would like to give to her daughter. I felt her regret and sadness at having not properly protected her children. She wished her daughter to know that she was deeply sorry she was not there for her when she was needed the most. She expressed to Allison that she loved her very much.

I felt her mother, prompting Allison to ask a question that had been bothering her for a long time. I could tell that this was a deep wound that needed to be brought up in order to heal. I encouraged Allison to ask her mother the question that she held in her heart. Through her tears Allison asked her mother, "Why did you not want me?". Instantly I was shown a vision. Allison's mother had a miscarriage prior to the birth of Allison and she suffered postpartum depression quite severely. When Allison was born her mother had a hard time bonding with her because she was afraid that she would hurt her as a result of her depression. She pushed Allison away out of fear that she would harm her daughter.

I sat still for a moment as I allowed this information to really sink in for Allison. Her mother then showed me a beautiful blanket that was in a box. She expressed to me her desire to see the blanket moved out of the box and displayed in a place of prominence. When I told Allison this she smiled and said, she had her grandmother's blanket placed in a box under the bed to protect it because it was so valuable to her. She told her mother that she would take the blanket out of the box and hang it on the wall for everyone to see. Her mother smiled in a gentle and approving way and stepped back into the light.

I felt a second presence come into the room this time a male presence. I believe this to be her father. I described to Allison a gentle man with a quiet nature and a smile. He was wearing cowboy boots and carrying an ax in one hand. She gasped, covered her mouth as she exclaimed, "That's my dad! That's my dad!" She was so excited that he had come through she began to tell me about her father and what a wonderful man he was. She told me that she still had the ax that he used to cut firewood for the family home when she was a child. Her father wore a pair of black cowboy boots all of the time. He gave me a message to deliver to her, "You are loved kiddo. Keep your chin up you are strong." Allison said to me, "That is exactly something my dad would've said and did say many times when he was alive." He quietly stepped back into the light content with having delivered his message and making his presence known.

There were many more things we discussed during the reading and I could tell Allison left that day feeling lighter and more at peace than when she arrived. What an honor it was for me to be a small part of her healing process and connecting with her parents.

HANNAH

Hanna walked in my door and the whole room lit up. Her energy was so strong it practically glowed. I liked her immediately. Sometimes you meet people, and your energies seem to connect. Hanna was one of those people. Earlier in the day when I was focusing on her energy and meditating, I felt a sense of anticipation about our session together as if we were both in for a great surprise.

As we sat down together to begin the reading, I had a hard time not staring at her. It literally felt like I was looking into my own eyes. It was a very strange feeling unlike anything I had ever experienced before. To be honest, it was a bit distracting. I was trying to keep focused on her and not the similarities between us. Later I would realize that this immediate bond I felt with her was necessary in order to travel down the path we were about to go. We were like best friends sitting at the table talking about her hopes and dreams.

I began our time together talking about medical issues I saw in her body. My ability to see energy moving and vibrating has given me a special understanding of when someones body is not well. I see the energy around them slowing down, sluggish and sometimes even stopping all together in certain areas. Their aura will change color and I can identify areas of their body that need help.

In Hannah's case I saw that her joints, particularly her hands and fingers were very sore and stiff and had limited mobility. I felt that this was a hormonal problem created by an excess of stress in her body. Hannah agreed with me, she did have very bad joint pain, particularly in her hands. She also told me she had hormonal imbalances ever since she was a teenager. She felt that it was getting worse as she was heading into her midlife. I advised Hannah to try and reduce the amount of stress in her life and to have her hormone levels tested for any deficiencies.

In my notes I had written down the phrase, "fun with horses" and the number "12". My sense was that there was a young girl, perhaps Hannah's daughter. She absolutely loved horses and would own her own horse by the age of twelve. The bond between her daughter and the horse would be incredibly strong and keep the young girl out of trouble in her teens. Hannah started laughing and told me, "You just nailed it." She did have a six year old daughter who was completely obsessed with horses. She kept telling her mom that she wanted one of her own. Hannah would explain to her daughter, she was too young for her own horse and maybe when she was twelve they would talk about it. I also sensed there was a young boy as well. I asked her if they were twins? I believed they were the same age, although, with very different personalities. She nodded yes, she had twins, and they were as different as night and day.

• • •

be bold

make-up
hiding

very hard
worker, almost
too hard...

fun w/ horses?
12

silver
truck

what next?

53

stable/solid

stress
related illness

mother moving
in?

Chinese herbalist "nanaimo"

I saw her son's energy and he did not have the confidence and vitality of his sister. Instead, it was apparent to me, he lacked self-esteem and felt he did not measure up to other people. It was almost as if he needed to perform in order to be accepted. He seemed lost, disconnected and a bit out of place. He felt like he did not belong. I learned from Hannah that the twins had been adopted when they were toddlers. The little girl was treated like a princess and the boy mostly ignored, prior to them coming to live with her. She had spent many years reassuring her son that he was more than enough and did not need to impress anyone. He was simply loved. I heard my guides tell me that the young man should become involved in martial arts. This was a sport where he would be compared only to himself and not others. Therefore, his competitive nature and need to please would be directed at his own progress and advancement. Hannah gasped in amazement. She put her son in karate a few years earlier, but he was just too young. The day before our session together her son had pulled out his GI and asked if he could be a ninja now. I guess the universe heard him loud and clear and communicated to his mother that now was the time.

Next, I asked Hannah if her mother was living with her at the moment. I felt strongly that if she was not yet living with her, she would be within the year. It would be a challenge at first. Her mother was very strong-willed, stubborn and believed she was never wrong. I told Hannah that although this would be a difficult transition it was the best course of action for everyone involved. In the end she would be grateful that she took her mother in, and their relationship would be strengthened because

• • •

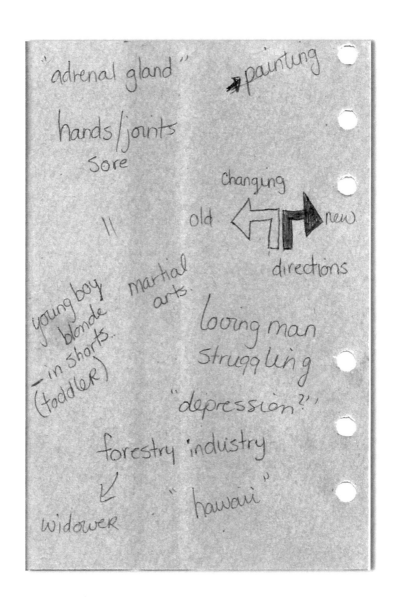

of it. Hannah's mother had recently been asking her if she could come for a visit. She was missing her family and wanted to come and stay for an extended period of time. Prior to me saying what I did, Hannah was avoiding the visit, but now realized that she should welcome her mother with open arms.

I could tell that Hannah was sitting in anticipation of something specific that she wanted to know. I knew that she had questions about her romantic life and this was the main reason for her coming in for reading. Sometimes, I will leave this type of information to the end of a reading because I find that once I start talking about someones lifelmate they tune out to everything else I'm telling them. I wanted Hannah to have a full reading and to give her guidance in all areas of her life not just her love life. Some may not agree with me directing the order of a reading. They believe it should flow naturally. However, in certain circumstances, I will use my discretion, with how I release information. Before I make the decision, I always ask my guides and God if this is the right decision. They have yet to give me bad advice.

I began to describe for Hannah the man that I saw coming into her life in the near future. He would be tall, over six feet, a large imposing man with a heart of gold. He would be gentle, romantic, a bit shy, stable and solid. I saw this man as loving children and open to having more even though his own children were grown. I told Hannah that he would have kind eyes, that he would love camping outdoors and that he worked in the forestry industry and was a widower. This man also struggled with depression his whole life, because of this felt unworthy of a life mate. His depression however, was not debilitating and he managed it quite well. Because of Hannah's compassion and understanding for others this would not become a barrier to their relationship. I knew that she would meet him by chance in a public place. She would need to be bold and be the initiator of the conversation. This was very outside of Hannah's character, but I sensed this was one of those situations where she needed to step outside of her comfort zone. To take a risk, walk up to this man and simply say, "I've been looking for you".

I saw tears forming in Hannah's eyes and she looked frightened. I asked her what was going through her mind at that moment. She pulled a piece of paper out of her purse and handed it to me. On the paper was written, "My soulmate will be: stable, solid, love kids, romantic, gentle, tall and muscular, love the outdoors, but most importantly have kind eyes." I got goosebumps from head to toe and almost started to cry. Hannah asked me, "Is this was real? Is this really going to happen? If my goosebumps were any indication, absolutely!

I believe this was the reason I felt such a sense of anticipation at the beginning of our reading. Hannah desperately wanted to know if this man she was hoping and dreaming for was just a fantasy or could possibly be a reality. I am certain that Hannah's willingness to put her hopes and dreams out there for the universe to fulfill is what brought her to me. Never be afraid to write down and have expectations for what you want. If you don't ask, you won't receive!

DEE

Dee was my first reading done over the computer. I was very nervous to say the least! I didn't know if my gifts would work the same if my client was not in the room with me. In theory I believed it would work. All of my information comes to me during my meditation times before I ever meet the person I am reading. I decided I was ready to push my abilities to new heights and explore different ways of helping people. I clicked the call button and logged on with Dee. As soon as I saw her, I knew that everything was going to be just fine. She was exactly as I had envisioned during my meditation time. Dee was a beautiful, strong and competent woman. After a brief introduction, we began the reading.

I began with an image that I had seen of a very large tree with deep roots and many branches some of which had decayed and were falling off. At the top of the tree was healthy new growth. I believe this image to be symbolic of Dees' family for many generations. I explained to her that I felt she had deep roots that went back many, many years. This long history and sense of identity were very important to her and provided her with a sense of pride in who she was. I also explained that along the way there were family members that were unhealthy and they fell away from the rest of the family. This was representative of the decaying branches on the tree. Dee

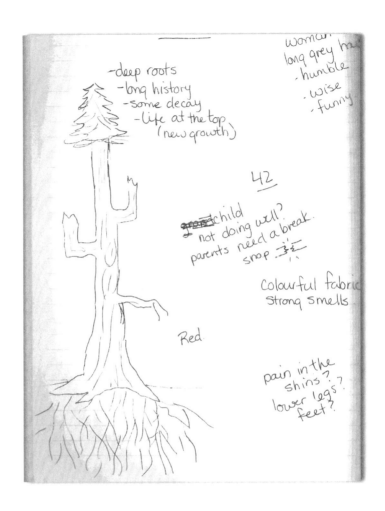

represented the new growth at the top of the tree. I explained to her, the choices she made in her life and within her family had brought new growth and wellness to her family tree.

I asked her if this resonated with her and was this was a good depiction of her lineage? Dee agreed with me.

• • •

41

She came from a very old family and her aboriginal heritage and her roots were extremely important to her. I drew another picture of mountains with a road going through a mountain pass. I believe Dee was meant to take a trip through a mountain pass to her homeland in the near future. This trip was for her and not for helping others. I felt she was becoming ungrounded and needed to reconnect with her roots. Dee said that she had not been planning a trip home, but the way home did travel through a mountain pass. She was feeling a bit ungrounded as she lived in the city far from her home. She would consider a trip home in the near future.

One of the other things that became very clear to me while I was reading Dee was that she was a mother to many. I felt that she had many children from many different nations. These children had brought much laughter, but also many tears. In particular, one child was not doing very well and Dee was at a breaking point with her. As I was talking Dee kept nodding her head in amazement. She had been a foster parent for many years, had many children and recently had adopted several children into her family.

Her daughter was going through a very difficult time and lashing out in anger. Dee had tried many things to help her, but to no avail. She was feeling at the end of her rope and had just said to her husband the day before, "I am ready to snap." I reassured Dee that this difficult time with her daughter was nearing an end and to hang in there. Her daughter was feeling frightened because she was getting older and almost ready to graduate high school. She was worried that she would be kicked out of the house after graduation. She had abandonment issues already and the thought of being asked to leave once she graduated was causing her intense pain.

I suggested to Dee, she reassure her daughter. She was in not going to be pushed out of the house before she was ready to go. She was loved and was a part of the family. Dee got quite emotional and expressed to me that this gave her hope and made perfect sense to her. She would absolutely reassure her daughter of her place in the family.

As we continued to talk about the family I drew her attention to my notes where I had written that there was a distance between her and her spouse. I asked her if she was in a time of separation or considering ending her marriage. I felt they were drawing farther and farther apart. I also felt this was something that had been coming for a very long time. Dee was already through the grieving process and ready to move on. Despite the ending of the marriage, she was feeling confident and ready for the next phase of her life. Dee told me that she and her husband had been living under the same roof but in separate rooms. He was moving out of the family home at the end of the month. She was feeling quite guilty because she was not upset about this, but rather looking at it with anticipation. I reminded her that she had been grieving this marriage for a long time and it would be normal for her to want to move on.

In my notes I had drawn a picture of five square boxes, in one of the boxes was a round peg. I asked Dee if she sometimes felt like a round peg in a square hole? I felt like this was pertaining to her work environment. Dee was a freethinker and very creative, but her workplace was

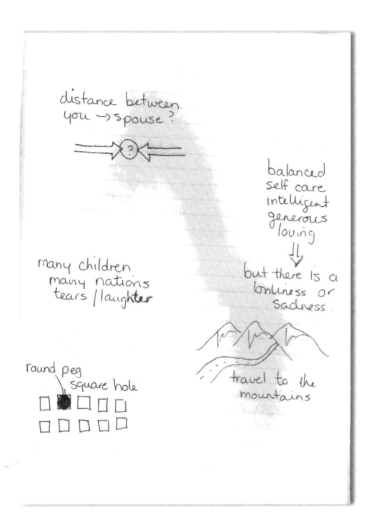

distance between
you → spouse?

balanced
self care
intelligent
generous
loving

but there is a
loneliness or
sadness.

many children
many nations
tears / laughter

travel to the
mountains

round peg
square hole

the exact opposite, full of rules and policies that did not make sense to her. I believed she would be leaving this job soon and moving into a more self driven position. Dee agreed that I had described her work environment perfectly and she had been considering moving on from there, but wasn't sure if it was the right decision. This decision was particularly difficult for her and was the thing she was most seeking guidance for during our reading. I reaffirmed for her to start looking for open doors and believing in her abilities. I felt that this new endeavor could literally change the world.

Dee would contact me for a second reading several months later. During that reading Dee was excited to tell me that she had changed jobs. She was much happier and feeling hopeful.

KELLY

Kelly was a young woman who came to see me because she was feeling stuck in her life and confused about the direction she should go moving forward. This is very common with a lot of my clients. We live in a society where people have lost the ability to trust in their own gut instincts and intuition. Their lives are so full of the constant flow of information, options and opinions. The attitude that everything should happen right now is pervasive in our society. All of these things can leave us feeling lost, just like Kelly was.

Once I explained what Kelly could expect during our time together and helped to put her nerves at ease we began the reading. I told Kelly I was going to get right to the heart of the issue and skip over some of the fluffy stuff because I felt that was why she was really there. She agreed with me and said that she actually was hoping that I wouldn't waste her time talking about silly things.

I saw a wall that she had around herself. It was an old wall, full of old bricks and mortar with lots of cracks and moss growing on it. I explained to her, this was a wall of protection she had been building up since she was a small child. At one time in her life, it actually served a purpose to keep her safe and protected, but it no longer served the same purpose. It was now hindering her and her current relationship.

Kelly had recently been thinking exactly the same thought, but she didn't know how to change and felt stuck. I explained to her, it was a slow process of making one choice at a time, to be a little bit more vulnerable, to trust a little more and to take risks when she felt safe enough to do so. These baby steps would eventually tear down the old walls that she had built up around herself and replace them with new healthy boundaries.

Next, I asked Kelly if she had been planning on moving? She laughed and said, "That's all I have been thinking about!" I shared with Kelly that I saw her leaving her hometown to move to a big city. This would be the best possible situation for her. Living in her hometown was very limiting and stifling. I also told her, she would be keeping her current job, but being transferred to a new location in the city. Kelly explained to me that a few days prior, her boss had mentioned a new position had come up in the city and would she be willing or wanting to relocate? This question stirred something deep inside of her, but also a lot of fear about the change. Would her boyfriend go with her? Would it be the end of the relationship? Would she be lonely? This was her reason for coming to see me.

I told Kelly that I felt she would be going to the city alone, but only for a short time. Within a couple of months her boyfriend would be joining her there. He had a very good job and was a bit nervous about leaving it behind without knowing if he would have a good job in the city. I reassured her his expertise was in high demand and he would have many job offers within a short period of time. She laughed and said that was exactly what he said when I asked him if he would be willing to relocate the city. I could feel a weight lifted off her shoulders as she began to see the possibilities ahead of her.

I had written my notes that Kelly and recently had a big, stressful argument. I asked her if this made sense to her. She said yes, she had just had a big argument with her

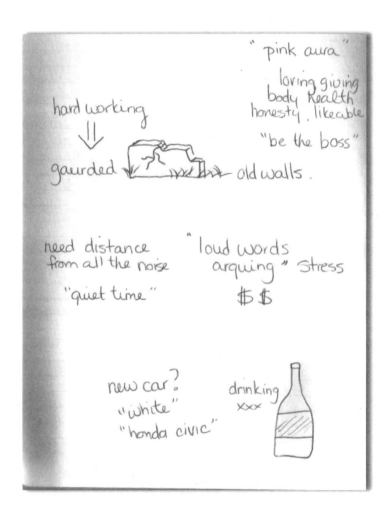

family the night before and decided she needed a break from them. The argument had nothing to do with her and yet, she was the scapegoat. This was a family pattern that repeated itself over and over. This made perfect sense to me as I also wrote that she needed some distance from all the noise, almost like a time out. I reaffirmed for her that she had made the right decision to take a break from all the family dynamics in order to focus on her own health and wellness and her direction for the future.

We talked a little bit about Kelly continuing her education once she moved to the city. I felt the direction she would be going in was holistic health and wellness and she should look for nighttime classes or something she could do online as she was going to continue to work throughout the whole time she was going to school. These were the questions Kelly had written down before we got together. Should she go to school and how that would work with keeping her job. I reminded Kelly that she already knew everything I was telling her. Her intuition was very strong, but she often second-guessed herself or talked herself out of what she knew was the right thing because of the fear of what other people would think. I encouraged her to stop making her choices based in fear and to start owning her brilliance. She would then attract more brilliance to herself. This brought a sense of vulnerability to Kelly. I saw her start to tear up and get quite emotional. I knew I had touched a nerve and so I gave her a moment to just process what I had conveyed.
During this break I felt the spirit of a young child come through. I knew this child was never born. When children pass away before birth, whether by miscarriage or abortion, they will show themselves to me as a five or six-year-old child. This makes sense when you think about

the communication because it would be very difficult for me to communicate with a fetus. Communicating with a young child who has language and facial expressions is much easier.

I asked Kelly if she had lost a child pre-birth. Through her tears Kelly told me a tragic story. She had been in a severely abusive relationship and found herself pregnant. The police, her family, and social workers had all suggested she have an abortion. Raising a child with this severely abusive man would be a big mistake. She was young at the time and desperately wanted to be away from her abuser. She went ahead and had a late stage abortion. She felt immense guilt from this event as it went against her belief systems and her values.

I felt Kelly's anguish and fear that she had made a terrible mistake. Fortunately her child had the exact opposite feelings. I knew the child was a little girl. She had red hair and dance in her soul. She loved Kelly deeply and knew from the moment that she was conceived she would never be born. She knew her role was to help Kelly separate from this man. It was a gift she gave to her mother at the expense of her own life. The young girl was so proud of Kelly for the life that she had built for herself and she wanted Kelly to know that she was dancing and singing in circles all around her. Through her tears, Kelly told me that she often heard humming and wondered what it was. Knowing that it was her daughter dancing around and protecting her brought her great comfort.

The young girl danced her way back into the light. In her place another beautiful spirit came. This one I felt was an elderly woman like a grandmother. In my notes I had written the words "sunshine girl" and "brings light and joy". Intuitively, I knew these words were tied to the spirit. I asked Kelly if she had a grandmother that used to call her sunshine girl. She gasped and said, "Yes, my granny called me that all the time." I told Kelly that her grandmother's energy was here. I felt that she had not passed away, but was still alive. I felt a separation between them. Her grandmother was still alive and Kelly had not had contact with her for several years. Her grandmother was a very religious woman and did not approve of Kelly living with her boyfriend or her other life choices.

I explained to Kelly, her grandmother's energy was coming through so strongly during the reading and was perhaps an indication to me, the time was right to reconnect with her grandmother and start healing. Kelly said she had been missing her grandmother a lot lately and maybe I was right. She was still concerned about any judgment that might come from her grandmother. I reminded Kelly, she is in control of her life and the choices that she makes. If she feels judged or threatened in any way, she can leave or set clear boundaries and try to create a relationship within those boundaries. Either way, she really had nothing to lose.

This reading really hit a chord with me because so many of Kelly's experiences were similar experiences in

feeling misunderstood

trouble expressing true self.

"want to be known"

pink ballett
   shoes - dance
in her soul.

☀ sunshine
   girl

↗ brings
   light ?
         joy

2ⁿᵈ job-self employment

health/wellness.

more school
nighttime
" /angara college "

my own life. With all of the people that I see on a regular basis I am always amazed that the universe brought them to me at the time that I need them, in order to heal myself as much as helping others to heal. I was blessed by Kelly's openess, vulnerability, her strength and her determination to create life her away.

• • •

SHEILA

$\mathcal{S}$heila was a beautiful woman with an open spirit and a fantastic attitude. I could tell right away that this was going to be a fun and very interesting reading. I began the reading really talking about the essence of who Sheila was and how I saw her energy. She agreed with me that I was quite accurate in my assessment of her personality and her traits. Her exact words to me were, "You couldn't be more spot on."

When I was focusing in on Sheila's energy I saw a distinct difference in the vibrational frequency around her midsection, particularly her stomach and uterus. The vibrational frequency was quite sluggish and the color surrounding this area was red. I asked her if she was having any pain or problems in this area? She replied, "Absolutely!" For quite some time she had been dealing with pain and inflammation in this area of her body with no relief for her symptoms." I expressed my belief that the problem she was having was caused by scar tissue from a previous surgery and she should have this looked at by her physician. This was a situation that could be quickly and quite easily remedied although difficult to diagnose. She agreed to go and see her doctor later that week.

During the time that I was focusing on Sheila's energy I kept seeing flowers and lots of them. I felt they were quite significant to her, but was unsure why. I asked her why flowers were so significant to her. Perhaps she had a tattoo or a memorial shrine or some special attachment to flowers. She started to laugh and told me that flowers were very significant to her. Her goddaughter had recently brought her a bouquet of hand-picked flowers and it meant more to her than any gift she could've received. When I asked her why flowers were so important to her, she said, "she had no idea, but they were her favorite expression of love." All of a sudden I had a flash of a past life that Sheila had lived.

As a Clinical Hypnotherapist, I often guide my clients into past life regression in order to find the source of issues they're having in their current life. Finding the source of an issue can be the beginning of the healing process. I am in a unique position being a psychic medium. I may have a vision of their past lives before they themselves see it during Hypnosis. I have to be very careful not to lead my clients based on what I've seen. My job is to guide them into discovering their past lives for themselves. In this case, we were in a reading and not a hypnosis session so I asked for permission to share with Sheila the past life that I had envisioned.

I had seen her as a young African-American girl, probably about six or seven years old. She was running through a field of wildflowers that were many different colors. She fell down in the middle of the field and lay on her back, taking in the smells and sensations of all the wildflowers around her. This was her escape from the hardships of living in poverty. As she lay there in the field of wildflowers I heard her mother calling her name, "Maise... Maise..." I could feel the young girl hesitated to leave her field of flowers knowing there were chores waiting for her at home. I expressed to Sheila that I felt

• • •

this past life was the reason she had such a special place in her heart for the gift of flowers. Sheila thought this was beautiful, it made so much sense to her and was very comforting.

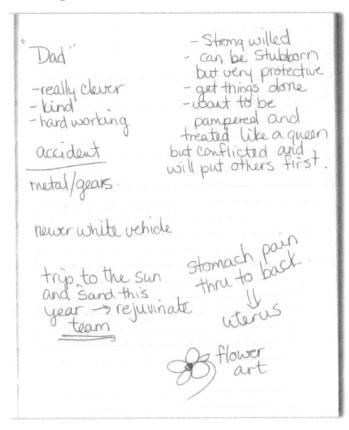

We then moved on to a few very specific items that had come up during my focused time. I had written down, "new white vehicle" and felt strongly it was time to sell this car. It was going to have some mechanical problems in the near future and would become a burden.

I asked Sheila if she had a white vehicle and was she considering getting rid of it? Sheila expressed to me that she had a conversation with her husband the day before about their newer, white, Ford SUV. She felt they needed to get rid of it quickly. He was not in agreement with her, but she was insistent. She wanted to get rid of it. My bringing it up in the reading was all the confirmation she needed to talk to her husband again. I told her it would take two weeks and she would have a new car. She chuckled, looked at her friend and said, "didn't I tell you it would be two weeks and that car would be gone.

I felt the sun shining down on my face and the sand between my toes. I felt completely rejuvenated, like the sun was feeding me energy. I asked her if she knew that she was a sun child? She needed the energy from the sun to refresh her and give her much needed vitality. I felt she would be taking a trip in November back to the sun and the sand. This trip would help to refresh her and her husband, who I saw as a strong team. Sheila had just recently moved from down south and was longing to go home. She had said that by November she wanted to make a trip back there to spend some time in the sun and the sand.

The energy in the room began to change and I could feel the presence of spirit come into the room. I asked Sheila if she was open to communicating with the spirit that had come in? I always ask for permission before I begin any kind of spirit communication. Just because somebody comes to see a psychic medium doesn't necessarily mean that they are ready for what I have to offer. Sometimes they need to trust me more before they are open to receive. In this case I had established a rapport

• • •

and a trust relationship with Sheila through the accuracy of my psychic reading and she was more than open to allow spirit communication.

I sensed a male presence that I would call a father, although I felt he was more like an uncle or a friend than a father. I described him as very clever, a survivor, able to get out of just about anything, people feared him although he was more of a gentle giant. I felt this man had died an accidental death. I could feel metal crunching under my head as if I had fallen from a distance and landed on something metallic. I got the letter "J" and saw corduroy bell bottom jeans. The type you would've worn in the seventies. This was someone who was very fashionable and laid-back. When I finished my description of the spirit, I looked up and Sheila was staring at me with a look of recognition. I was connecting with her dad and he was more like an uncle or a friend than her father. He was a very casual guy and also a very young father. The physical description as well as the description of his personality were accurate. His name was George. No "J" but definitely the same sound. She explained to me there was some mystery around how he died. The authorities were not sure if he was poisoned, drugged, if it was self-inflicted, or a heart attack. He had fallen and hit his head on the metal faucet in the washroom.

Now that we had established this was her father, I asked him if he had any messages for his daughter. His message was, "I want you to know that I don't want you to know. Just trust me." Her father knew she wanted to know the details of what happened and how he died. He felt it would in no way make her life better and it wasn't information he wanted her to have. It was the whole

• • •

57

reason she had come to see me. To get the answer to how he had died and to know that her father was on the other side. Sheila understood her father was able to see immeasurably more than she could ever imagine and had a wisdom about what was best for her. She should trust him. Sheila began to cry and told me that she had been carrying around the burden of his death for sixteen years. She could finally let it go.

I gave Sheila a moment to continue connecting as her father's energy was still present in the room. I asked her if she had any questions or anything she wanted to ask her dad about? She wanted to know if he saw her son or her daughter? Were they going to be okay? George told me he really liked her son. He was very sarcastic and smart mouthed and alot like his grandpa. He told me his grandson played sports where he was often hurting himself. He was very clumsy. He also told me, he would keep the boy safe and always be there to protect him. One day her son would make an absolutely fantastic father. He would be very patient and playful and Sheila would be incredibly proud of him.

Just yesterday Sheila was watching her son interacting with friends and she turned to her husband and said, "Doesn't he just remind you so much of my dad?" She confirmed that he did play many sports and often hurt himself. She was pleased to know that her father was keeping him safe. Sheila got goosebumps all over when I told her that her son would be an amazing father. She mentioned she had recently seen him playing with a friend's child and she had the exact same belief he would be an amazing father one day.

• • •

As for Sheila's daughter, George told me she was unusually beautiful. He called her, "a step above". He instructed Sheila to be very protective over her. She was somewhat socially awkward and could perhaps find herself getting into difficult situations. He gave me the letter "A" and I asked Sheila if her daughter's name had this letter in it. She gasped and told me her daughter's name was, "Alison."

I could sense George moving away from me. I looked at him to say goodbye. He turned towards me, flashed me a peace sign and a big smile and was gone. Sheila laughed with me and exclaimed, "That is so like him, he was a real cool dude."

People often ask me why don't my loved ones tell me something really important? Why do they talk about silly things so much? I respond by telling them, when we cross over to the other side the true essence of who we are, our spirits or souls don't change. If we were sarcastic and witty in life, chances are we will be the same in spirit. It is important to remember that our loved ones retain their true nature. However, their perspective does change. When they are in spirit they can see everything. Time has no meaning and they are not encumbered by the things of the physical world. They do have a special wisdom and it is best to trust what they share as being exactly what you need to hear, when you need to hear it.

JANE

Jane travelled a great distance to come and have a reading with me. I knew right away that our session together would be very important for Jane. I was overcome by a deep sadness during my meditation. The sadness saturated her energy. I instinctively knew she was grieving the loss of someone dear to her. As she sat down across from me, I sensed her nervousness and hopefulness at being able to connect with her loved one. That type of expectation can put alot of pressure on me. Although I can communicate quite well with spirit, I cannot always control who comes through in a reading and who doesn't. When I feel pressured, I have to remind myself that I can only do what I can do. I have to leave the rest up to God and the spirits.

I typically start readings with my psychic predictions and my sense of who the person is. However, this was no typical reading and I decided to launch right into connecting with Janes' loved one. I'd written down in my notes that Jane should be working through her sadness slowly and at her own pace. I told Jane that there would be many people in her life telling her it was time to move on and to get on with life. Her grief was her own and she should take as much time as she needed. Regardless of what others around her were saying. Tears began to well up in her eyes. She nodded her head and agreed with me, people had been telling her it was time to move on but she just wasn't ready. By giving her permission to continue grieving, she felt weight lifted from her shoulders.

There was a male presence surrounding her constantly. I asked Jane if she had recently lost her husband. She was unable to speak, and nodded her head.

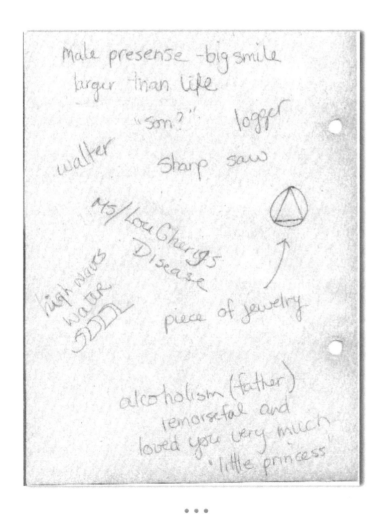

I began to describe the man that had come through. He was a big man with a big smile. I sensed he had a larger-than-life personality, very funny and gregarious.

I'd written in my notes that he was a logger or worked in the logging industry. I saw a very sharp saw with a large blade, the kind that they would use to cut up big timber. Jane confirmed that her husband worked on the rail system that would move the heavy logging equipment back and forth between the logging camps. She had seen this type of saw many times. She was overwhelmed by the description of her husband and said she felt as if he was standing right there. I explained to Jane that he was right there, and that he was always right there. He never left her side.

He began to show me images of his last few days. He had suffered a degenerative disease that slowly ate away at his body. I'd written in my notes, "MS/Lou Gehrig's disease." It was difficult for Jane and their children to watch this larger-than-life man slowly fade away. He wanted Jane to know that he was no longer suffering and that he was watching over her and the children. I also got the sense that in life, Jane and her husband did everything together. They never spent a night apart and were very deeply in love. Janes husband was also a jealous man, but not in a bad way. He was jealous over the woman he loved and protected her fiercely. He expressed to me that he was not yet ready for Jane to move on with her life. He knew there would be a time that she would need to move on and he was okay with that, but just not yet.

Jane laughed at that because she knew her husband so well. They had conversations about his passing and his desire that he would not want her to move on with her life because of his deep love for her. She said that sounded exactly like something he would say. His presence was palpable all around us. I asked Jane if she could feel him. She said she did sense him all around her, and at times thought she was going crazy. I reassured her that she was not going crazy and that her husband's energy was very strong.

I had drawn a circle with a triangle inside of it and felt it was a piece of jewelry that Jane owned. It seemed significant and I asked her about it. She knew exactly what I was talking about and explained to me it was a piece of memorial jewelry she had made with her husband's ashes. I thought this was a beautiful expression of her love and wanted her to know that her husband was very pleased and liked the jewelry.

He began to show me images of hummingbirds fluttering around the yard where they lived. He wanted Jane to know that the hummingbirds were a sign from him, he would always be there protecting and loving her. Jane was taken aback by this. She had been noticing hummingbirds all around the yard and recently purchased some feeders. They'd never had hummingbirds before and she wondered where they had suddenly come from.

He asked me to hold Janes hand so he could feel her touch and she would know his touch once again. I'm not sure how spirits experience physical touch. What I do know, is when spirits ask me to touch their loved ones, I experience a rush of energy, goose bumps and often strong emotions. As I held Janes hand, she felt the emotion too, and her grief let go. We sat like that for some time as I gave her space to experience the feelings. After a time I felt her husband's energy leave. I took in a deep breath and refocused myself back to the current time and place.

work through the
sadness . . . slowly.

Carol

doll floppy in
the corner
Raggedy Ann?
Grama made or
gave

hummingbirds
are a sign for you.

daughter:
keep dancing

I asked Jane if she was okay to continue on with the reading. I felt there was more information that needed to be shared with her. She nodded her agreement and we carried on. I picked up on the energy of her daughter who I felt was a great support for her throughout this difficult time. The exact message I was given was, her daughter needed to keep dancing even though she may not feel like it. The physical act of dancing would help in her healing process after the loss of her father. I could see her daughter with the music cranked up high, dancing around the house and just being silly. Jane said that was something her daughter used to do regularly and hadn't done for quite awhile. I encouraged Jane to tell her daughter that it was time to start dancing again.

As our time together was winding down I felt a lightness in Jane that she didn't have when she first came in. Seeing this positive change in my clients is one of the reasons why love what I do. Helping people to feel lighter and more hopeful is a feeling I cannot describe. I have to say it's pretty awesome.

Jane would come back to see me several more times. My ability to connect with her husband on such an intimate level was a tangible way that Jane could feel connected. Sometimes, I struggle with whether or not it is healthy for people to continually try and connect with people that have passed over. My concern is that they will stay locked in the past and not move forward to live in their present.

My final session with Jane was very different than the previous sessions where she had come to connect with her husband. In this session I could tell that

. . .

something was different about Jane. She had a sparkle about her that was not there before. She did want to connect with her husband again, but this time it was to ask him if it was okay for her to move on with her life. She had met someone. Her husband came through that day to give his blessing for the woman he loved to love another. It was one of the most beautiful moments I have had the honor of being a part of. I wish Jane nothing but the best and the happiest future for her and her family.

PART 3

RANDOM COMMUNICATION

ROMANTIC DINNER

If there's one thing I know from dealing with spirits, it's just when you think you have it all figured out, they change the rules. Earlier, I talked about my God Goggles and how I can turn my ability to see spirits on and off. I have learned there are exceptions to everything. Following are a couple of experiences I had while trying really hard to not have experiences. As you will see, when spirits have an important message they will find a way.

On this particular day, my husband and I were out for a nice romantic dinner. We don't get to do this a lot. When we do, I try hard to remain completely focused on him and not the spirit activity going on around me. Tonight spirit had different ideas. As we were eating our dinner, I was distracted by a beautiful spirit woman who was standing just behind a couple sitting across the restaurant from us. I tried desperately to ignore her and keep my focus on my husband, but she was very persistent. She kept staring at me and tapping her foot, beckoning me to come over. I expressed to her this was my night off and I needed a break, but she would not let up. My husband, who is now very tuned in to me and my abilities, could tell that I was distracted by spirit. He looked at me and said," Oh for crying out loud, just go over."

I walked over to their table as politely and inconspicuously as I could. I apologized for interrupting their dinner. The woman stared at me and with the strangest look on her face she said, "Is this a Teresa Caputo moment?" I laughed at the comparison but sheepishly admitted, yes it was. She said, "I just knew it. You have been staring at me all night long. I knew there was something going on." Talk about embarrassing! You think I would get used to walking up to random people and telling them what I see, but I really haven't. Every time spirit prompts me to act, I will usually do it, but always with a little trepidation.

I explained to her I had seen a woman standing behind her. I described the woman as in her sixties, with beautiful gray hair cut in a very stylish bob. She was made up, dressed very well and even had her nails done. This was a woman who took great care in her appearance. She was extremely impatient and pushy. She was running her fingers through her hair and looking at me as if to say, "Hurry up and get over here. I don't have all day." The woman I approached knew immediately who I was describing. I politely asked her not to tell me what she knew until after I had delivered the message to her. I explained the spirit woman wanted her to call her sister. Although I knew this was not her actual sister, but a friend who was very much like a sister. They had been estranged for some time. The spirit was adamant that she call. She knew the two of them were both very stubborn and would not want to be the first one to break the long silence.

The woman began to cry and was unable to speak. Her husband explained to me that they just had a conversation before dinner about this particular friend. He was encouraging his wife to call her and break the silence. Her response was, "If she wants to talk to me, she can call me."

The spirit who came through was the mother of this woman's estranged friend. She owned a hair salon and was a very stylish woman. She was also a very stubborn and impatient woman. I had described her perfectly, right down to the color of her nails and the style of her hair. Her husband looked at me and jokingly said, "You got anything for me?" I laughed and replied, "Nope, I got nothing." It broke the tension of the moment and we all had a good laugh. I went back to my table after giving her one of my business cards.

A few weeks later I received an email from the woman in the restaurant. After our exchange, she reached out to her friend. She was shocked to learn her friend had cancer and was terminally ill. She didn't want to call because she didn't want her to think the only reason she was calling was because she was dying and wanted sympathy. They laughed with each other when they realized they didn't even remember why they weren't talking in the first place. They reconciled had many laughs and were able to be together in her last days. She thanked me for being bold enough to come over and give her the message that day.

I am grateful that this spirit was so persistent and didn't allow me to ignore her. Sometimes there are situations that are simply bigger than us and more important than what we are doing. The healing that can come is profound and truly miraculous. I feel blessed every time I have an opportunity to be part of that.

BOY IN THE DRIVEWAY

Another experience that I had quite randomly one day would bring healing not just to one person, but to an entire family. I was at a friends' house one day and we were standing out in the driveway. I was just getting ready to leave. I asked her what she was up to that day and she told me that she had to go and visit a friend who had just lost her nephew unexpectedly and tragically. Quite suddenly, I felt the presence of a young man standing beside her. My friend; Hannah, looked at me and asked, "Are you seeing something? You are staring off in the distance." I told her I believed that her friends nephew was here and was she open to hearing what he had to say. She encouraged me to communicate with him.

I began to feel agitated and couldn't stand still. I kept moving from side to side. I described him as approximately six feet tall, lanky, wearing work boots, jeans and a big smile on his face. I felt that he was a very hyper person that couldn't sit still. He told me he'd passed away in a car accident. He said to me, "I didn't even know I was tired." I heard a repetitive sound like a thump, thump, thump. I sensed this sound had somehow lulled the young man to sleep. A few moments later, I saw a dog appear beside the young man.

I asked my friend if any of this made sense to her? I told her I believed the dog passed away in the car

• • •

73

accident, but not until a few days later. She stood in front of me looking completely stunned and said, "Yes, the young man had died in a car accident and his dog passed away a couple of days later." She asked me if the young man had any messages for his family? He said, "Tell his mother that he would not leave her until she was completely ready for him to go." He also told me he hated the picture the family was planning on using for his memorial. He didn't want them to use it. He would be in the flickering candles not the picture. He shared with me a few more details and then left. He would come back to me several times over the next couple of weeks to share more information. After the experience, I was quite tired and went home to rest.

The next day Hannah called me and she was freaked out. She kept asking me "How did you do that?! How did you do that!?" I asked her what she was talking about and why she was so upset. She wanted to know about the picture, how did I get rid of the picture? I had no idea what she was talking about. I was confused and asked her to calm down and explain to me exactly what had happened.

The family had posted a photograph of the young man on Facebook to announce the memorial service to all of his friends. That morning the photograph had been removed and a video of a flickering candle was in its place. The framed photograph that they intended to use at the memorial service had also disappeared and no one knew where it went. I was starting to understand why my friend was so frantic! I was amazed at the ability of this young man to manipulate the physical realm simply because he didn't like that photo.

● ● ●

Hannah went on to explain that she had shared what I told her with the young man's family. His mother was overwhelmed. She felt a sense of relief. There was some question as to whether or not the young man had caused the accident or unknowingly fallen asleep at the wheel. She explained that her son had a sleeping disorder and would often fall asleep at random times. When he would wake up, he would look at his mom and say, "I didn't even know I was tired." This was confirmation for her that he had fallen asleep and not intentionally driven his truck off the road. They also found a large rock stuck in the back tire of his truck and I believe this was the thump, thump, thump noise that I heard.

I cannot explain how this young man's spirit could have manipulated Facebook and made the photograph disappear, but I know that he did. He was strong and clear and really wanted his family to have answers. He would communicate with me on several other occasions, providing accurate information and bringing healing to his friends and extended family.

• • •

BOY ON THE BEACH

Every once in a while when I am going about my daily business, a spirit will make themselves known to me. There is not always a clear reason why or what they need. I have found, that if I choose to engage with them, the reasons always present themselves. This is one such case.

My husband and I were taking our dogs for a walk on the beach. It was a beautiful warm sunny day. We were beach combing, looking for sea glass and driftwood like we often do. We had our heads down, searching the ground for little treasures. As we walked through one particular area of the beach, I felt a shiver go through me with a definite change of temperature in the area. Because of my experiences with spirit, I knew this meant there was a spirit near me. I lifted my eyes, put on my God Goggles and looked around.

Sitting on the beach directly in front of me, I saw a little spirit boy digging in the sand. He seemed frantic as he dug. He was desperately looking for something. I sat down on the sand beside him and watched for a moment. He became aware of my presence, looked at me and asked, "Can you help me find my necklace? I've lost the silver cross that my mommy gave to me. She will be very mad if I don't find it. Can you help me find it?" I told the little boy that I would do my best to help him. I sat down and began to dig with him.

In the back of my mind, I thought to myself, wouldn't it be amazing if I actually found a silver necklace in the sand! What would be the odds of that happening. We sat together, digging for probably ten minutes, but there was no necklace to be found. Not my lucky day I guess.

My husband, who is used to these unusual occurrences happening; noticed me talking on the beach and digging in the sand. He himself is an incredibly intuitive man. Knowing I needed some space, he took the dogs and continued walking down the beach. I just love this man and how he handles paranormal occurrences like they are no big deal. I turned back to the boy and explained to him, his mother was waiting for him on the other side. She most likely wouldn't care if he had the necklace or not. She missed him and wanted him to be with herin Heaven. I told him I could help him to cross into the light if he was ready. He was absolutely insistent that he could not leave the beach without the silver cross necklace. I tried again to have him crossover and again he refused. I felt there was nothing else I could do for this boy. I stood up, wished him well and continued my walk down the beach.

When I joined my husband farther down the beach I felt unsettled. Somehow there must be something I could do to help this little boy. All of a sudden I had an idea. My guides will give me ideas when I am least expecting it. I knew this was my guides helping the little boy. They suggested I take two pieces of driftwood, remove the ponytail holder from my hair and fashion a cross out of them. Then, I was to take one of my sterling silver earrings that I was wearing and hang it on the cross.

• • •

It would not be a sterling silver cross, but it would be a cross with sterling silver.

This all sounded like a great idea, but these were brand-new earrings and not cheap! I was not very excited to part with one of them. I explained to my husband what I felt I needed to do in order to help the little boy crossover. He said, "Absolutely, you have to do that!" As we walked back towards our vehicle, we came upon the spot where the little boy was sitting digging in the sand. I sat down beside him again and I gave him the wooden cross with the silver earring hanging on it. I explained it was the best I could do. I felt that it would be good enough to make his mother happy. He smiled the biggest smile. His whole face lit up and in the next moment he was gone. I knew that he had crossed over into the light to be with his mother now that he had his silver cross.

My husband and I sat for a few moments on the beach to feel the lightness in the space that he left. We gave thanks for the gifts that I'd been given. We got up to leave, walking the same way we had come. I looked down and rrght in front of me were three beautiful shells in a straight line, laid out just for me. These shells were not native to the beach that we were on. They were not there when we came through the first time. I believe this was the little boys' way of giving me a gift to honor me for giving him a gift. I still have those shells and they remind me to keep my eyes open and my heart soft. To remember to use my gifts to help the spirits around me find peace and be with their loved ones.

LUNCH WITH KATHLEEN

Kathleen was a young woman who had passed away suddenly and tragically. She decided to make herself known to me during a lunch date I was having with a friend. She was clearly in distress and wanted to deliver important information to me, the event unfolded like this...

My girlfriend and I went to a little restaurant for lunch and we sat down at a table that was up against a brick wall. We ordered drinks and began to look at the menus. All of a sudden, I heard a blood curdling scream and felt complete panic and terror. I looked at my friend and asked, "Did you hear that?" She replied to me, she heard nothing but she noticed that I had jumped in my seat and was looking panicked. It took me a moment to get my bearings. I took a long, deep breath and tried to refocus my energy on the menu. Again, I heard a terrified scream and realized this spirit was not going away.

My friend looked at me and wondered if I was okay? I explained to her, I was hearing a young woman screaming and felt that she wanted to communicate with me. My friend encouraged me to do what I needed to do. My gift was important and never try to shut it down. I focused in on the energy of the young woman and immediately I was given several words. I wrote the words down on my phone; Kathleen, motorcycle, murder, Legion, yellow. My friend watched as I wrote these words down. She asked me if I knew what they meant? I had a pretty good idea, as the spirit, whose name was Kathleen, had shown me how she died.

I believed the young woman had been murdered several years ago by an older man. He was a boyfriend that she had broken up with. He rode a motorcycle. He was devastated by the break up and began stalking Kathleen. I felt he was the one responsible for taking her life and she was violently murdered, late at night. I wasn't sure what the word, "Legion" or the word, "yellow" meant. Perhaps it may identify the victim in some way. I also felt the young woman was connected to the building that we were having lunch at. I was not originally from the area. I didn't know the history of the building or any past crimes that had been committed in the town.

My friend had lived in the town her whole life. When I spoke about what I had seen, a look of shock registered on her face. She stared at me across the table and said, "Kenna, I know exactly who you're talking about and what happened." She began to tell me the story of Kathleen. She was known by all the locals as "Kathy". She was a young woman who worked in a business directly beside the restaurant where we were having lunch. She had been dating a much older man who, coincidentally, rode a motorcycle. She had broken up with him shortly before her death. He was investigated by the police but no charges were ever laid because of a lack of evidence.

My friend also told me that on the other side of the building where Kathy had worked was the local Legion. She would go after work most days with her

. . .

boyfriend to have a drink and unwind. The day of her death, Kathy had been at a friends' wedding. She was wearing a yellow dress.

I wondered to myself why Kathy was coming through now if all of this information was already known. What was she hoping to gain. Before I could think about this for too long my friend said to me, "It's interesting that she is coming through now, as just last week her case was reopened and her ex-boyfriend was charged with the murder because of new DNA evidence. He confessed to her murder."

The universe has this amazing way of lining things up in the exact right moment, in the exact right place, with the exact right people so that messages can be received. If I had not been in that restaurant, on that day, with the person that I was with; that message could have been misunderstood by me. As divine guidance would have it, Kathy received justice and was able to finally communicate exactly what had happened to her on that terrible night.

LITTLE OZZY

One final story I will share with you happened many years ago while I was attending church. During my time in the church I would often get visions and words for people. My pastor trusted my gifts and allowed me the freedom to express myself. On this particular Sunday, I kept getting a strong sense that I had a specific message for someone in the church. I stood in front of the congregation and announced, "I believe someone here today will know I am talking to them when I say, I have a message from the baby. If you believe this to be you, please come and find me after the service. I will share with you the message." I heard a woman in the back of the church gasp and begin to cry. At the end of the service I went to her and sat down beside her. I asked her if she thought my message was for her? She nodded her head as she was unable to speak. Her husband was holding her hand and she wept silently. I explained to them, I get visions and words for people. Would it be okay if I shared with them. They agreed and I began to describe for them what I had seen.

I saw a young boy about three or four years old with blonde hair, freckles, and big brown eyes. He had his arms out to his side and was running around the house pretending to fly, while listening to heavy metal music. He had so much joy in his face. I could tell that he loved that type of music. This was unusual to say the least, as I don't know many toddlers that rock out to heavy metal. The boy's father explained to me that their son had passed away when he was four years old. His nickname was, "Little Ozzy". He loved listening to Ozzy Osbourne's music. I focused in on Little Ozzy and asked him, what was the message he had for his parents? He told me to tell his mother, "You fed me well." I thought this was an unusual message and wasn't even sure I should tell her. I didn't want her to worry that I may think she neglected her child. But again little Ozzy insisted I tell her, "You fed me well."

I shared this message with the family. The mother fell to the floor sobbing uncontrollably in such deep anguish and grief. Her husband knelt beside her rubbing her back and comforting her. Saying to her, "This is why we came. This is why we came. You needed the healing. This is good." I gave them some time to absorb what just happened. When they were ready, they came over to me and shared with me the significance of that message.

Little Ozzy had a heart condition and had stopped eating and was getting very weak. His mother had tried making him every kind of food she could think of. Trying to get him to eat. He was not able to eat anything she made for him. A short time later he passed away. The mother had blamed herself for many years. Believing that if she had just found the right food, he would've eaten and he would have lived. His message absolved her of guilt that she had been carrying for over ten years.

They had never gone to church before. That morning over breakfast they had looked at each other and said, "I think we should go to church today." I never saw

• • •

them again, but I know they were meant to be there that day to receive the message from their son and finally have the healing they longed for. I wish them all the best and know Little Ozzy is always looking out for them.

In each of these situations spirits pushed through and persisted until they were heard. I am so very grateful for the gifts that I've been given. For being a medium to help facilitate such deep healing and communicate messages from the other side. I never take it for granted and considerate it the highest honor.

• • •

PART 4

HOUSE CLEANSINGS

FOREST HOUSE

One of the services that I perform is house cleansings for people that are having challenges with energy and spirits in their homes. Often times when people have unexplained phenomenon within their homes they believe a ghost or spirit is haunting them. I have found this is rarely the case. Most of the house cleansings I have performed are really just a matter of clearing old residual energy from the space as well as releasing earthbound spirits into the light. Occasionally, if the spirit does not want to leave the property I try to find a solution that will work for both the homeowner and the spirit to be able to live in harmony together.

On this day I found myself negotiating a deal between the homeowner and the spirit of the previous homeowner. I'd gone to the home at the request of the owner. She was having difficulty in certain areas of her home. There was an uneasy feeling and a cold, drafty energy. Her daughter was feeling uncomfortable in her bedroom because of paranormal experiences she had in the room. She felt a general sense of uneasiness. I began my work in this part of the home. I also picked up on the same feelings as soon as I entered the room.

I moved on to a room in the basement that was colder than all the rest. The homeowner explained to me that no one ever went in this room because it made them so uncomfortable. I asked to be left alone in the room. I wanted to try and connect with the energy that was there.

I was surprised when a spirit man showed himself to me. I described him as a large man with a big beard and the hands of someone that worked hard all their life. He was very unhappy. He had been a solitary person in life and enjoyed the privacy and quiet of his property. He was particularly proud of all the beautiful trees on his property and enjoyed the privacy it gave him. He felt very at home in the forest. When I asked him if he would be willing to move into the light and allow this new family to take over the home he became agitated. He told me, "They can leave. I am staying." I decided to change the subject and began a conversation with this man about his life, his family and his passing. I told him a little bit about the family that was living in the home and how they loved the property and look forward to raising their children there.

The spirit man told me that he was very upset with the family. When they moved in, they cut down most of his trees and the yard was now exposed to the street. I thought about this and realized, if it was my home and I valued my privacy I would probably feel the same agitation as this man. Sometimes when dealing with spirit you have to be very creative in finding solutions. I asked the man if the family were to plant a tree in his honor and apologize to him would he be willing to allow them to live there in peace? He thought for a moment, looked at me and with a smile in his eyes said, "That would be nice."

I thanked him for being so understanding and told him that I hoped he would be happy living in peace with this wonderful family. I then explained the

• • •

compromise we made to the homeowner. She agreed that this was an awesome idea and a great compromise. She would plant a couple of trees and apologize to the spirit man.

I followed up with her about a month later to see how things were going at the home. She had planted trees outside the room in the basement where the spirit resided. He could now see them from his window. Her family apologized to the man and asked for his forgiveness. Since then, they have had no more disturbances in the home. The uneasy feeling they felt before was gone. They were now sharing their home and more than happy to do so.

This was a wonderful experience for me. So often we focus on getting rid of the spirits. In this case, I was able to create harmony by leaving a spirit in place. Why he didn't want to leave and go into the light was never understood by me. Then again, there's a lot I don't understand about the spirit world. Every adventure brings a new understanding of how things work on the other side.

VINTAGE HOUSE

I was called to the 1950s' vintage house because the current tenant was experiencing some paranormal activity. He wanted to know if it was attached to him or to the house. When I arrived I walked around the house, recording any impressions I received. I was drawn to the garage. There was a window high up in the garage wall. I sensed that this garage was not original to the house, but a later add on. Where it now stood, there used to be a large oak tree. I also knew that the spirit in the house would frequently rattle the window and even open it at times. This was very unusual because the window was so high in the wall and it would have been very difficult to reach without a ladder.

When I entered the home to begin my walk around I was joined by a very nice spirit man in his fifties. He revealed to me that he was a master craftsman and had done most of the detailed and extravagant woodwork throughout the house. I believed him to be a friend of the current tenant. He was very proud of the work his friend was doing to maintain the home in it's beautiful condition. He would even oil the bannisters and trim.

I felt pain in my lungs and saw black spreading in that area. This is often an indication of cancer spreading. I asked my client if he knew who this spirit could be? He said, "Absolutely, it is my best friend, and roommate. He did all of the woodwork in the house and recently passed

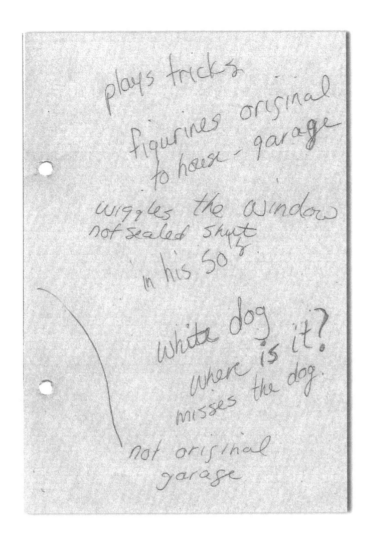

plays tricks

figurines original
to house - garage

wiggles the window
not sealed shut

in his 50's

white dog   it?
where is it?
misses the dog.

not original
garage

away from lung cancer. I miss him terribly and wondered if it was him that was rattling and opening the window in the garage. He used to complain that it never closed properly"

This was a great start to the house cleansing and really set an open and receptive mood for the rest of my work. I sensed several spirits throughout the home and believed most of them to be attached to the tenant himself. I saw a wall of photos, a memorial of the people he had lost over the years. One spirit, I believed to be his mother, instructed me to tell him it was time to take the shrine down and let go of the dead. He needed to start living again. This was a strong and emotional message and I was not sure how my client would receive it. Grieving is a very unique process and everyone has their own timeline.

In this case, he was ready to hear the message. He led me to the wall that had the photos of his lost friends and family. He said he was afraid to take the pictures down because it might mean he would forget them. I suggested he take his time and when he was ready to begin the process of letting go. I reminded him that his mother loved him very much and only wanted the best for him.

We took a few moments to gather ourselves and then proceeded to the basement. The air in the lower part of the house seemed thick and heavy. I moved into a room that was large and had a beautifully designed parquet wooden floor. As I admired the floor, I began to have a vision of several people crammed into this room. There was loud music, lots of drinking and partying. I saw a large pool of dark, red blood spread out on the wooden floor and seep into the cracks. The party stopped and never started again. My client told me the house used to be owned by a large corporation. It was used for management and employees when they were in town. The house was known to be a regular party house in town. The company abruptly stopped using the house after one of the party guests had slipped on the wooden floor, hit their

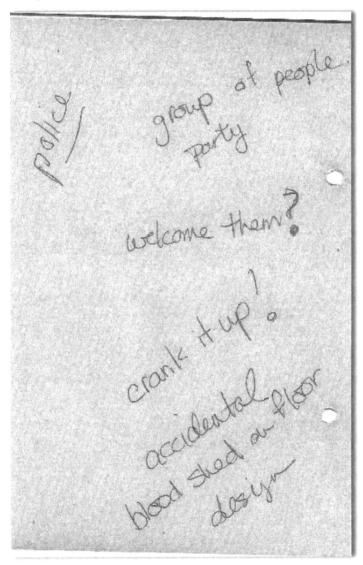

head and passed away. The house had sat empty for years. My client's friend had bought the house and lovingly started restoring it up until his recent death from cancer.

Together we prayed over the house and blessed it. We released all of the residual energy and made peace with any spirits that were there. My client said he felt ten years younger already. He would start to take down his memorial shrine. I learned a lot about grief from this gentleman. Our loved ones want us to live our lives and not get stuck in the past, but at the same time, they are so loving they stay with us for as long as we might need them to.

WATERFRONT HOUSE

 he waterfront house is one of the most
spiritually active homes I've been to. I began having
supernatural experiences before I even entered the
building. Over the years I've gotten used to the different
way spirits communicate with me. I can sometimes get
almost a bit blasé about it. I forget the people with me are
not as comfortable or familiar with these experiences.

Just prior to going to the waterfront house to do
the cleansing, I was out for a drive with my husband. We
drove by the house and I pointed it out to him. I told him
this was where I would be doing the house cleansing. A
few moments later, the stereo in our car was cranked up
to full volume without either of us touching it. This had
never happened before and really frightened my husband.
He shared with me that he felt energy, like a lightning
strike, go through his body and exit through the steering
wheel immediately before the volume on the stereo
cranked up. He asked me what I did to him and what the
heck just happened?

I realized this must have been very unsettling for
him. I tried to explain the energy he felt was most likely a
spirit that was using him as a conduit to communicate
with the electrical system of the car. I felt the spirit was
trying to scare me away from the house and did not want
me coming there and doing a cleanse. This type of
interaction is harmless, but I can see how it could freak

people out. Lucky for the homeowners the spirit did not scare me away. The experience had the opposite effect, and I was excited to see what was to come.

I sat in my vehicle in front of the house to get a sense of the energy there. I wanted to discern any spirits or residual energy before I entered. When I do house cleansings, I ask my clients not to give me the address until just before I am  meant to arrive. I can give them a much truer reading if I have less information. Being human means that sometimes my ego gets in the way. The more I know about a place, the harder it is for me to put my own thoughts and beliefs aside and allow spirit to work through me. Once at the home, I will meditate, take notes, do grounding exercises and protect myself before I ever go inside.

This was a very large home that was roughly one hundred years old. It was three stories high and had many additions to the original structure. As I sat meditating and looking at the house, I became aware of a spirit in the top floor window of the house. I saw a woman who was cloaked in black, but her face was completely white with no features. She was standing in the window and it appeared to me she was on guard.

• • •

I began to smell smoke and felt very panicked. I looked to the third floor and felt as if I was falling. I could hear footsteps running up and down the stairs. I saw a

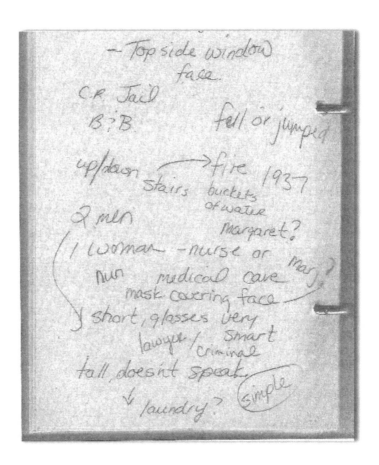

man who had a slight stature, and wore glasses. I got the sense that he was an incredibly intelligent man and held a position of power, possibly a doctor or lawyer. These types of visions are like being transported inside of a movie. Everything else around me fades away and I am completely engrossed in the vision. Once I had written all of this down in my notes, I decided it was time to enter the home.

I met with the lovely woman who lived there. I explained to her the process of what I would be doing. I asked her not to tell me anything about the house or any experiences that she had been having. To simply let me walk through the home and share with her my impressions. When I finished going through the entire house, we would then sit down and discuss everything that had been revealed. It is important once I start house cleansings that I stay in the right frame of mind and allow my energy to connect with spirit. If I am drawn into conversations it is difficult to stay connected to spirit.

I walked through the house and I experienced many visions. Sometimes it can be difficult to tell the difference between a spirit that is connected to a home and residual energy that is left over from previous residents. The easiest way for me to tell the difference between the two is, whether I can communicate with them. With residual energy it is very much like watching a scene unfold. They are completely unaware of me and unable to communicate. On the other hand, a spirit is aware of my presence and often tries to communicate in one way or another. In this house I would experience both residual energy and spirit communication.

I began my tour in the basement. As I walked down the stairs, I saw a vision of a man and woman having a big fight in the main room. They were yelling and screaming at each other. I got the sense the argument was over money. I saw a young child sitting in a playpen crying. The man had an angry outburst and struck the woman. Next, I saw police lights and heard sirens. Then there was nothing but silence. I intuitively knew that this was residual energy left over from an event that had

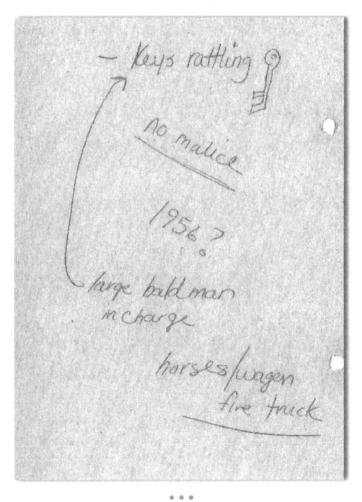

happened recently. I shared the vision with the homeowner. She proceeded to explain, the scene had unfolded in the basement exactly as I saw, but it had happened the previous week. She had a family member staying in the basement with her boyfriend and baby. They had indeed argued over money, he struck her and was arrested by police. The homeowner stated that things had felt unsettled ever since.

I suggested we do a cleansing and a blessing of the space in order to clear out the negative energy and restore the space to positive and calming energy. She was in agreement with the idea and we did this together, pushing out the darkness left behind and filling the space with light.

We then moved to the main floor. I walked around recording observations I had and any images or impressions I received. I saw the spirit of a large man wearing a uniform. As he walked, I heard what sounded like keys jangling. He seemed to be in charge and had an air of authority about him. He walked from room to room following me around. He never engaged with me and was unresponsive to my attempts at communicating with him. I believed this was not an active spirit, rather residual spirit energy again. I made note of him in my journal and kept going.

As we climbed the stairs to the top floor, I felt a noticeable change in the temperature of the house. I stopped in front of a closed door. I discerned this had been a problem area for the family. I felt the door was being locked and not opening, possibly trapping someone inside. My client confirmed for me, her three year old

• • •

daughter had been locked in the room on several occasions, from the outside. On one of those occasions the mother was unable to get the door open and had to call a neighbor for help. I saw blood and asked if this person injured themselves trying to open the door? She explained, he had to drill a hole through the lock to get it open. The drill had slipped and cut him quite badly.

I sensed these door locking incidents were related to the spirit lady with the black cloak and white face. I took a moment to refocus my energies and attempted to

communicate with her. She came to me as soon as I asked her to come forward. She seemed anxious to talk to me. The spirit woman explained to me, the house was not safe for little children and she was doing her best to protect the child. This was why she was locking her in the bedroom. I explained to the spirit woman, her protection was very much appreciated but no longer necessary. The little girls' mother would protect her from now on. The spirit seemed pleased to know the child would be safe and she faded away. The homeowner was relieved to know this spirit would no longer be a problem.

We finished up the house cleansing and blessed the home. I always do follow up and research after visiting a property. This gives confirmation to the homeowners. It also gives me the opportunity to be sure there is a positive change in the activity in the home.

I went to the local museum and archives to research the property and learn its history. What I found out was truly shocking! The building had been the original jail and courthouse in the area. I was able to find photos of the original warden in charge. He was a large imposing man that would carry the keys for all the cells! This lined up with the spirit man and the jangling keys that followed me around the house. The slight, intelligent man I had seen when I first arrived turned out to be the town's only physician. He lived right next door to the jail with his wife and young son. One fateful night there was a fire in their house and his young son died. He had been tossed out the

window to waiting firemen. The sound of footsteps I heard, were most likely the fireman running up and down the stairs trying to put the fire out.

The spirit woman I had seen in black on the top floor was one of the nuns that would tend to the prisoners in the jail. I found a photo of one such nun and the habit she wore obscured her face almost completely just as I had seen!

When I did the follow up appointment with the homeowner she was amazed by the confirmations I had uncovered during my research. She expressed her gratitude and wanted to let me know the energy in the home was much lighter. There had been no further issues since my session. In homes with a long and rich history there is always a story to tell. This home was certainly no exception!

RIVER HOUSE

When I am asked to do a house cleansing I never really know what to expect. They are all so different and always exactly what they need to be. At the River House I became aware that it was not the house that needed my attention as much as the homeowner. When I arrived at the property I was moved by the great energy in the home. It was in a very peaceful setting. I felt as if I was standing on Holy ground. I would later discover during my research, the house was actually built on property once owned by the Catholic Church!

I sat down with the homeowner to discover why she wanted me to come. She expressed her frustration over not being able to sell the house, despite excellent conditions in the real estate market. She felt perhaps, the house was cursed. I was pretty sure it wasn't the house that was blocking the sale. More likely, the owners unrealized anxiety and fear about what her future would hold, were holding back the sale.

We began the walk through and came to her bedroom. I was drawn to a beautiful wooden dresser with a large mirror on the top. I felt the spirit of an elderly woman attached to it. I asked her if she had any message for my client. She told me she was her grandmother. She had left a special message, just for her granddaughter, hidden somewhere on the desk. Grandma wanted her to know she was there and giving her blessing for the future.

• • •

104

She wanted to remind her granddaughter to love herself more! Later that week my client would contact me to tell me that she had found some numbers etched into the back of the mirror that she had never noticed before.

Sacred ground.

old lady?
lonely.

Carl Feeney
Carlton

Mark - valentines
car accident
cousin
mother mental ill
Young family (lueres cancer)
Birthday Party balloons
Grama's dresser
love yourself
dance naked in front of mirror

Even though, she had owned the dresser for several years. She believed the numbers to be her grandmothers' phone number from when she was a child.

We went from the bedroom into the living room where I was greeted by the spirit of a man. He told me his name was, "Mark". He had known my client when he was a young man. I described him and told my client what he said. She told me she knew only one Mark but hadn't spoken to him in years. She didn't know if he had passed on. I asked her to focus on him. I would ask him to give me more information to confirm his identity. He began to show me images of roses, Valentine hearts and boxes of chocolates sitting on a desk in a classroom. This was an unusual image and I had no idea what he was trying to say.

It is important that I don't try too hard to interpret the images and messages I am given by the spirits I communicate with. I am a medium and my job is to deliver messages exactly as they are given or risk messing up the true message. I told my client exactly what I had seen. She leaned against the wall for support. She had been asking Mark to show me the Valentine gifts he had given to her. It was truly him. She was overcome with shock at the clarity of his message, but also sadness at the knowledge that he had passed on.

His message was simple. He had a very difficult home life as a child and his adult life had not been much better. He wanted my client to know, she had been a bright light in his world. He always felt great affection for her, and appreciation for her kindness towards him. He was at peace now and no longer struggling. My client

• • •

never expected to have this person come through, especially in the way he did.

It was exactly what she needed to be reminded of at that time. She was leaving a difficult relationship where she felt unloved and mentally abused. Her reason for selling the house, was to have a fresh start and find a way to love herself again. Perhaps, even find another man to love in her future. The appearance of her grandmother and old boyfriend were exactly what she needed as the encouragement to move forward. Her house sold shortly after our time together. I am pleased to say that she has moved on with her life in a new town and is very happy!

HOUSE OF SECRETS

This house I called the House of Secrets because when I arrived at the rural sprawling property I knew there were many secrets concealed here. There was two houses, a large garage and a good sized property. The area was remote and secluded. When I did my initial walk through of the buildings and grounds, I had an uneasy feeling. Was I getting involved in something I shouldn't be?

The homeowner greeted me and told me, "Just do what you do and then come find me." This was a bit unusual. Most of my clients like to stay with me and observe as I do a walk through. I respected his desire to stay distant from the process and knew it would become clear to me later why he chose to keep his distance.

I went to the rental house first and met his tenant. They had experienced several paranormal incidents in one certain area of the house. He wanted to leave me to see if I could identify and resolve these issues. I was drawn to two bedrooms at the rear of the house. In one of the rooms, I felt there was an opening to the spirit world that needed to be blessed and sealed. This type of rift or opening can occur naturally or can be the result of people playing around with the paranormal without proper care and knowledge. I had a revelation of things hidden in the attic of this house. These items were left here by the previous owners and needed to be removed. I felt a criminal intent behind the items. In the second bedroom, I had an entirely different feeling. I was aware of an extremely religious energy that was harsh and judgmental. I saw a teenage boy lying in his bed, feeling confused and conflicted about his beliefs. He was torn between a strict religious upbringing and his First Nations cultural beliefs.

The tenant was amazed I had identified the opening in the room and the hidden items in the attic. He said he couldn't explain to me why just yet, but I was bang on. The teenage boy I had seen was his son. His ex wife was a Fundamentalist Christian with strong views she was teaching to their son. The young boy was really struggling between love for his mother and staying true to his tribal beliefs. I suggested to the boy's father, he be consistent with him and always answer his questions truthfully and without malice. The boy would eventually figure things out for himself.

I made my way back to the main house and garage. I was drawn to a particular spot in the backyard. The area was currently a beautiful green lawn, but I knew at one time there had been a fire pit in the middle of the yard. I saw a vision of several men standing around the fire and they were burning things. It felt as if they were concealing incriminating items. There was an air of somberness about the scene. As quickly as the vision came, it was gone. I was left wondering what other secrets I would uncover here. I moved into the garage space and sensed a disturbing energy of violence coming from beneath my feet. This didn't make sense to me. The garage was a large cement slab with seemingly nothing beneath.

I entered my client's main residence and headed towards the back of the house where his bedroom was located. I believed this to be the area where most of the paranormal activity was occurring. I could envision the window coverings moving, clothes falling off hangers and a knocking noise. I sensed this activity was in some way attached to the homeowner himself and not the house. I wrote all of this down to discuss with him when I was done my assessment. In the living area of the house my attention was directed towards an ancient artifact hung very high on the wall. I focused on the object and asked my guides and God for more clarification as to why this particular object had jumped out at me. I didn't have to wait long for an answer. I was shown an ancient aboriginal tribe using the object in a ceremony. It had strong spiritual energy and was placed so high on the wall, it was asserting power over the space. I believed there was more to the story of this powerful object and couldn't wait to ask my client about its origins.

I asked him to come upstairs so that we could discuss all my findings and come up with a plan to move forward. We sat down, and I explained everything I had uncovered in my time there. I asked him if he was aware of the history of the property or its previous owners? He appeared a bit reticent to discuss anything. I knew he had called me to help him and I encouraged him to release the secrets from the home. I knew he wanted to move forward with a clean slate and deal with the paranormal activity.

He began by telling me the property had originally been owned by a notorious gang. They had used the property to conduct business. He also admitted that he was a part of this gang and was tasked with being the caretaker for the property. He was aware of many secrets and was shocked at how many I picked up on. There was a drug operation in the tenant's house and most likely there were left over items in the attic that he would dispose of right away. I described exactly where the burn pile was in the yard, where the gang would dispose of items. He had recently planted a new lawn hoping to cover up the ugly burned area.

Recently, he had discovered a secret door that was buried under the earth and a slab of concrete. It appeared to lead into a basement below the garage, he never knew existed. He chose not to go into this hidden basement, but admitted most of the disturbances around the property began when he exposed the hidden doorway. He was no longer associated with the gang and wanted to leave that part of his life behind. This was why he called me.

He had a feeling that his own past and troubles may have been part of the reason for the activity around his home. He wanted to know what he could do to rid himself of the negative energy and spirits he had allowed into his life. I talked with him about some daily cleansing rituals he could do. I suggested he forgive himself and make better choices moving forward. I also performed a house cleansing and blessing.

My client told me he had a long family history of being on the wrong side of the law and confessed that his great grandfather had been a grave robber. The artifact I was drawn to was stolen from an aboriginal burial site over a hundred years earlier. He had tried to return it, but was unsuccessful in his attempts, so he kept it. I advised him to move the object to a lower place on the wall and suggested we apologize to the aboriginal spirits. He agreed to try it. We sat quietly while I connected with these ancient spirits. I walked him through how to apologize and make amends, offering to keep the object safe and respected. The ancient ones were appeased and appreciated this man's humility and willingness to change.

My client thanked me for the work I had done for him. He felt better already. It was as if a great weight had been lifted from his shoulders. I have learned from personal experience in my life that holding on to the past and beating yourself up for mistakes you have made never really turns out well. A few weeks after my visit I was made aware that things had settled down at the property and my client was continuing to grow and heal.

• • •

PART 5

THINPLACES AND BEYOND

WHAT HAPPENS WHEN WE DIE?

I was sitting outside in the most inspiring and serene forest to begin writing this chapter about what happens when we die. I saw some movement to my right. I try to be as mindful of my space and where I am every moment so I don't miss any messages. On my right, there were three large ravens sitting on a branch watching me. I had been in that area for many days and had seen many little birds. This was the first time I had seen ravens. They make a unique sound that is throaty and hollow. In my life ravens have been symbolic and especially when there are three grouped together.

I must admit that writing this chapter was making me quite anxious. It is such an important subject, often controversial and can change a persons perspective or faith. I felt daunted by the task of sharing what I know and have experienced. I am intensely aware of the scope of the afterlife and how little we truly know. My Christian background, relationship with God and my ability to communicate with spirits of people crossed over, can be a challenge to reconcile. The things I have learned and intuitively know do not always line up. This was where my apprehension came in.

When I saw the ravens this morning it spoke to me as a sign. I have a message to share and although, not everyone will agree with my experiences, there are also many people that will be impacted in a positive and hopefully life changing way. I am mindful of what I share. I share from the heart and a desire to bring hope and light to a sometimes dark and hopeless world. I am also awake to the truth that just when I think I have this all figured out, it changes!! I will do my best to shed some light on our afterlife.

From a very young age, I knew that spirit people were real and interactive with me. I have twelve spirit guides that have been with me since childhood. When I was younger, I didn't know what they were. I knew that they were there when I needed an escape or someone to talk to who understood me. They were my teachers. By the time I was in grade two I realized this was a unique relationship I had with my friends and that the other kids did not have such friends. I was a smart girl and really wanted to be like the other kids so I kept my spirit friends for myself. To be honest, I kind of liked having them as my special secret all to myself.

When I was in my teens I started to think that something was wrong with me and tried desperately to make them go away. I began having other spirits, both positive and negative intruding on my life. It was overwhelming and scary and made me feel even more misunderstood and different that everyone else around me. At sixteen years old I tried to take my life for the first of many times. I am eternally grateful that my misguided attempts to make the voices and attacks stop were unsuccessful.

I spent most of the next decade trying to numb myself and my gifts with drugs and alcohol. When my son was born, I tried very hard to have a fresh start and learn to live with the unique abilities that I had to communicate with spirit and see vibrational energy. It was a difficult time of my life that I often refer to as, the dark years. Although I struggled I was also set upon a path of self discovery and acceptance.

All of these experiences have shaped who I am today and what I have learned about what happens when we die. I personally have had several near death experiences as well as being present when a number of my loved ones have crossed over. I have also been incredibly blessed to be present when new life has been born into this world. From an energy perspective, the process of birth and death are remarkably similar! The rush of energy and the peace filled sensations that overtake me are the same.

For some, death can seem like a very scary process. My experiences with death have been some of the most beautiful moments in my life. Please do not misunderstand. I am sensitive to the sadness and grief of losing a loved one. I have grieved and lost more people than I would like. My intention is to give a different perspective. I have conducted hundreds of readings where I have connected and communicated with spirits. Some have crossed over into the other side and some have stayed in what I call, "the waiting room".

My years of talking with these beautiful souls have educated me on what happens when we die. Human beings are body, mind and soul. We consist of a physical body, our minds and our spirits. When we die our physical bodies can no longer hold our minds and spirits. The energy that is our essential being leaves this physical world and transcends into the spirit world. I call it, "Heaven". Others may call it "the light" or "the other side". People have many names for this universal energy, for consistency and in keeping with my integrity, I will refer to it as Heaven.

Heaven is open to everyone! There are no exceptions to this rule. We all have free will. We are given a choice to go to Heaven or not. If you choose not to go into Heaven, I do not believe you are going to Hell. It is my understanding there is a dark spirit realm, but it is inhabited by demons, not humans. In my life I have been visited by many dark entities over the years. I have learned some wonderful techniques for protecting myself from this kind of influence which I have shared in the reference section of this book. I will not give much space to this subject in my book because it serves no purpose in bringing light, only fear. I only mention it to relieve any misunderstanding that we will go there if we are not nice people. What does happen if we choose not to go to Heaven? Why would people not want to go to Heaven?

When we pass over we go to the Waiting Room. When we get there, we are given a choice to carry on to Heaven or to stay in the Waiting Room. It has been my experience that there are many different reasons why people will not cross over right away or sometimes never cross over at all.

When someone dies suddenly or unexpectedly they will often have a harder time crossing over because they don't understand that they are deceased. It may take some time for them to come to grips with what has happened. Often times, a loved one who is in Heaven will come down and get them. They will gently explain what has happened and invite them to cross over. If a person feels there is unfinished business in their life they may delay crossing over until they feel there has been a resolution. If a person had an attachment to things, money, addictions or people, they may have a difficult time letting go of the physical world. This can often result in paranormal activity or "hauntings" as spirits stay connected to their possessions or loved ones. People who have strong religious views may have difficulty crossing over because they feel unworthy, they have not done enough to earn their way in or perhaps they think they are not good enough. Let me say again, there is nothing we can do to earn our way into Heaven. We are given a choice to continue our lives in spirit form, growing and learning. Much of what I do is help spirits to cross over and continue on in their evolution into pure energy.

My clients often expect that when their loved ones cross over that they will become omnipotent, wise and angelic spirits. It is often a surprise when Uncle Joe comes through with the same sarcastic sense of humor he had in life, talking about his old 57 Chevy! We will retain much of our personalities, likes and dislikes, hobbies and mannerisms when we pass. What we gain is a universal understanding. Time has no meaning and spirits can look back over their lives with a wisdom they did not have in life. We are essentially given a do over! Messages from loved ones can be as mundane as talking about a dress you wore that they particularly liked, to apologies and regret over mistakes they made in life. I have never been able to figure out what messages will come through or

• • •

119

why. I do understand that they are exactly what is needed at the time it is needed.

Another pertinent subject I get asked all the time is whether or not someones deceased loved one will be their guardian angel? I do believe that we are assigned guardian angels at certain times in our lives, but in my experience they are rarely someone we knew. Rather, angelic beings that have never been in physical form. We are also blessed with spirit guides. These are spirits of people who have passed over and have chosen you as an assignment. They want to grow and learn through you as much as you do by listening and learning to trust in them. I believe the reason our loved ones are not our guides is because it is far too personal for them and they may not always be able to guide you on your own path. They may try to influence you with what they think is best for you. Our guides are always concerned with our best interests and will never suggest we do anything that is harmful to ourselves or others.

Thinplaces exist all around us. Do we have eyes to see them? I would define thinplaces as being objects, places or moments where we feel very close to our Creator and the spirit world. My favorite thinplace is under a giant willow tree, in a park in beautiful Victoria, BC. Every time I go there, time seems to melt away and I am deeply connected to God and Heaven. The rest of the world just fades away and I am captivated by the intense energy of this place. When I am doing readings I am purposeful about creating a thinplace to make communication easier. I do this by raising my vibrational energy and opening my eyes to see. Often times a certain object will have thinplace energy attached to it. Simply holding the object will make you feel closer to your loved ones. I want to encourage you to be watchful for the thinplaces in your life and spend a few moments there in the light.

Every time I practice my mediumship and have the blessing of being able to connect and communicate with spirits, it is always fresh and new! There is so much we don't understand about the spirit world and I don't think we are meant to. We all have an innate desire for knowledge and understanding. I have come to believe we are given as much as we are given because of the great wisdom and knowing of our Creator. I am exploring and evolving in my knowledge of what awaits us every day. I am also happy to be firmly planted here on this gorgeous earth with the most amazing people.

LAST THOUGHTS

We are living in a wonderful time of spiritual renewal and a deep thirst for understanding. Why are we here? What is the point? Am I really making a difference in the world? Is there more to this life than just what we see? We are crying out for meaning and purpose. It seems to me, as we get smarter and more advanced the less answers we are able to find. There is a real movement towards mindfulness and gratitude. We are longing for a kinder, gentler existence and have less tolerance for the ignorance and hatred all around us. I know that I myself have asked these same questions and searched for answers that made sense. I do not pretend to have the answers, but having asked the questions has certainly given me a greater understanding than before.

Life in this world continues to move forward as it does in the spirit world. I hope through the stories and experiences in this book you will know, these two worlds are joined forever together. In the thinplaces we can reach through and connect the two worlds. Know that when your loved ones pass on, they are not gone. The essence of who they were in life, lives on in spirit. No matter your particular cultural beliefs, religion or spiritual understanding; we are all body, mind and spirit. My goal in writing this book was not to convince you of anything. Our own individual experiences will shape our particular lessons. I hope that I have answered some of your

questions, dispelled misconceptions and encouraged you
to be your own unique self, full of light and love!

"Our deepest fear is not that we are inadequate.
Our deepest fear is that we are powerful beyond
measure. It is our light, not darkness that most
frightens us. We ask ourselves, "Who am I to be
brilliant, gorgeous, talented, fabulous?" Actually,
who are you not to be? You are a child of God.
Playing small does not serve the world. There is
nothing enlightened about shrinking so that other
people won't feel insignificant around you. We are
all meant to shine, as children do. We were born
to make manifest the Glory of God that is within
us. It's not just in some of us; it's in everyone.
And as we let our own light shine, we
unconsciously give other people permission to do
the same. As we are liberated from our own fear,
our presence automatically liberates others."
Marianne Williamson

Imbuing an Object with Intention:

Hold the object (candle) in both hands and visualize it being infused with brilliant white light from your hands. Just the same way you would do the white light protection. But this time see the energy soaking into the candle and making it glow bright white. You can state an intention out loud if you want to;

"I infuse this candle with powerful purifying energy and ask that this energy spread through our lives and remove all negativity."

Then when you light the candle, it releases the energy out into your home, and by extension, the universe.

Working With Angels and Guides:

The process is very simple,

a) Just pray to God (your interpretation of the Creator) that you would like to work more deeply with your angels and/or spirit guides and ask that they come and introduce themselves to you.

b) Visualize yourself surrounded by powerful protective white light,

• • •

c) and then sit quietly in meditation and see what happens. You may get a feeling of presence with you immediately, or you may not. You may hear a voice or see things in your mind that are related to your guides. Most often, they will come to you a bit later, like in your dreams, or late at night before you fall asleep.

d) Keep a journal of any information you get about them, like their appearance, their name, or anything else you can pick up. This process can take some time, so be patient. Working with our guides is a very subtle experience at first. They come in very quietly and wait for us to notice them, rather than "barging" into our lives.

If you don't pick up any information about them at first, don't despair, just keep working at it every day, and they will eventually introduce themselves to you.

House Cleansing Ritual:

You will need:

*one white taper candle for every room in the house
*plus one for each entrance to your house
*Myrrh, Sandalwood or Sage incense   --
*Holders for the candles and incense
*Sandalwood oil
*a chalice of water
*sea salt

Prepare a chalice of warm water and dissolve some sea salt in it. Take a shower or bath, but before you begin washing, hold the chalice of salt water in your hands, and "charge" it with white light. Ask to be purified of all negative energies and entities. Pour the salt water over yourself, from head to foot. Visualize white light energy removing all negativity. Then continue with your shower like usual. After drying off, anoint yourself with the oil (on brow, heart, and each shoulder). Ask for white-light protection from the Goddess, and visualize white light surrounding you.

Anoint each candle with the oil, starting from the base, up to the top. Set one candle (and one stick of incense) in each room of the house, and one at each entrance to the house. Prepare another chalice of warm salt water. Walk through your house with the salt water, sprinkling it thoroughly in each room, being sure to get some into corners and closets, behind doors, anywhere negativity can gather. As you sprinkle, you might chant something like;

"Negative energy may not stay, I release it and send it on its way. Negative energy, I banish thee, and as my word, so shall it be!"

Say this with confidence and power in your voice. Continue sprinkling salt water in every possible area of your home. Once you've finished that, light the candles and incense. (Be sure they're not near anything flammable!) Let them burn all the way down. While they are burning down, sit in a quiet location and visualize white light energy infusing every room of your home.

Doing this ritual every few months will leave a calm, cozy feeling in your house. You can also place dishes (or make sachets to hang) of protective herbs around your house. Lavender flowers, fennel seeds, and basil work well at keeping negativity away.

Cleansing & Smudging the Body:

Hands: To cleanse what we touch and to touch all things in a gentle and kind way.

Eyes: To cleanse our sight so we see all things that are good and to look at others in a kind way.

Nose: To cleanse or sense of smell so we know the things around us through smell.

Ears: To cleanse our ears so we can hear all things in the best way and find the goodness through anything negative.

Mouth: To cleanse or words so that we may speak in a kind and non-judgmental way.

Head: To cleanse our mind so we may think clearly and in a kind and gentle way.

Feet: To cleanse our steps so that we may step lightly and kindly on our mother, the earth.

Back: To cleanse our troubles and lift the weight away.

Tools for Growing Your Psychic Gifts:

I firmly believe that everyone can develop and grow their natural psychic and intuitive abilities. It takes a commitment to practice and learn to trust yourself. We all have that "gut feeling" but we have been influenced to ignore it or second guess that voice. Practice, trust and testing are the keys to increasing this natural ability within us. Following are a couple of exercises I have learned over the years that you can use to discover your own psychic intuitive skills.

Cards:

- Using a normal deck of cards turned face down. Begin to flip them over.

- As you do begin by listening to your instincts and guessing whether the card is black or red. Keep track of your accuracy on a piece of paper.

- Be careful not to overthink it or second guess your choices. Just let go of your conscious thoughts and trust yourself.

- When you feel ready you can then go on and identify what suit the card is following the same practice.

- With practice you will begin to see your percentages rise. Don't be discouraged if you are getting a growing percentage of the cards wrong!! This is also an indication of a psychic gift. Growth is growth!

• • •

Dice:

- This is like the cards exercise. Using a single dice and a cup.

- Put the dice in the cup, shake it and turn it over. Before lifting the cup use your intuition to discern the number on the dice.

- Keep track of your answers and watch your progress grow!

Meditation:

Meditation of any kind is a powerful way of learning to let go of your conscious thinking and tapping into your subconscious mind and your intuition. There are many options available to learn and begin to practice meditation. I have recorded some self-hypnosis meditations to help grow your psychic and intuitive skills and these are available for purchase on my website;

www.psychickenna.com

Link to Spiritual Protection Meditation:

https://soundcloud.com/user-973948090/spiritual-protection

Psychic Journaling:

I journal my psychic impressions every time I meet with a client and it is a very helpful tool in tapping into your natural aptitude. My suggestion is that you choose a specific person (this person can be passed over or still on this side) and meditate for at least 15 minutes just focusing on their energy and essence.

Intuitive/Psychic Journal

Date:_____

I Focused On:_____

I Saw:_____

_____

_____

_____

_____

_____

_____

I Heard:_____

_____

_____

_____

_____

_____

_____

I Felt:_____

_____

_____

_____

_____

_____

_____

_____

Messages & Symbols:_____

_____
_____
_____
_____
_____
_____

Contemplations:_____

_____
_____
_____
_____
_____
_____
_____
_____
_____
_____
_____
_____
_____
_____
_____
_____
_____
_____
_____

Clinical Hypnotherapy with Kenna Smith CHt.

GROW YOUR

PSYCHIC AND

INTUITIVE SKILLS

www.psychickenna.com   Mindful Action

Hypnotherapy

Clinical Hypnotherapy with Kenna Smith CHt.

PRACTICE

SPIRITUAL

PROTECTION

www.psychickenna.com Mindful Action

Hypnotherapy

Clinical Hypnotherapy with Kenna Smith CHt.

CREATE

ABUNDANCE

IN YOUR LIFE

www.psychickenna.com Mindful Action
Hypnotherapy

Clinical Hypnotherapy with Kenna Smith CHt.

CREATE

BALANCE

IN YOUR LIFE

www.psychickenna.com

 Mindful Action

Hypnotherapy

For further information on Kenna Smith, CHt.,
seminars, videos, self-hypnosis audio, to book
for your private event or to schedule a personal
reading;

please email:

psychickenna@gmail.com

or go to the website:

www.psychickenna.com